A Time to Dance

a Silverton Lake Romance

Diana Lesire Brandmeyer

DKD Books

O'fallon, IL 62269

DKD Books
PO Box 487
O'fallon, IL 62269
www.dianabrandmeyer.com

to my someone

Never run from fear, but into it because God is with you all the way. Ann.

...a time to mourn, and a time to dance;...

Ecclesiastes 3:4

Never run from fear, but into it because God is with you all the way.~Ann

A TIME TO DANCE

CHAPTER ONE

A moving truck swerved in front of Deni Sparks' Jeep, coming within inches of her front bumper. She slammed her foot against the brake pedal. Heart thumping, she smacked the horn. "Please don't let the man behind me require introductions and an exchange of insurance cards, God."

Traffic bumped through the pockmarked potholes of the St. Louis Poplar Street Bridge, slowed to a crawl, and then stopped. Ahead of her, a bridge patrol tow truck squeezed through the snarled traffic with its yellow lights blinking.

"There is nothing like a stalled car, a flat tire, or a wreck to start your Saturday morning off right way." Deni checked the mirror for the telling red splotches that always appeared when she was anxious. Here neck was strawberry red. Of course it was and likely to stay that way if she didn't control her frustration. She groaned. She hated being late to anything.

She picked up the letter lying on the seat next to her, as if by reading it, she could change the time of the meeting. The time on the paper remained the same. Ten o'clock at the law office in Belleville. She tossed it back on the passenger seat and bumped the air conditioner fan down a notch to combat the untypical June heat and humidity. "Please, God, make this traffic move or grant me extra patience."

She glanced over at the river. Through the passenger window she watched as a barge pushed upriver through the muddy Mississippi making better time than her. The traffic in front of her snaked into the left lane. Flipping on her blinker, she looked over her shoulder. The driver in the next lane waved her over. Another glance at the clock on the dashboard. Ten minutes to cover twenty miles. She pushed on the accelerator and sped toward the Belleville exit and to the answer to why she needed to be at the reading of Ann's will.

Deni drove around a fountain and turned left on Washington Street. She squeezed her Jeep into the parking space in front of a brick Victorian building. In the small front yard, an iron and gold sign that proclaimed Abernathy & Abernathy Law Offices swung in the warm breeze. She'd made it, and almost on time.

What had her grandmother's best friend Ann left her that required her presence at the reading? She gathered the letter and her purse. *Please God don't let anyone be upset that I'm here. Ann's relatives should be inheriting whatever it is, not me.* She sucked in a deep breath and opened the door.

The gentle breeze twisted her skirt around her ankles as she read the tiny print on the parking meter sign.

"The meters are free on Saturday."

Startled at the deep voice, Deni turned and found her focus centered on a chest. A manly chest. A strong looking—I can protect you from anything—chest. She tilted her head back and found herself lost in eyes of brown caramel. "I didn't want to take a chance. I'm from Missouri."

He flashed a dimpled smile at her before walking away. "Welcome to Illinois."

"Thanks." She whispered under her breath, "Friendly town." Deni watched his tanned, muscular calves flex as he walked. She didn't look away until she no longer saw the blue of his shirtsleeve as he slid into the sleek, black sports car parked two meters down.

Shoulders back she turned and faced her destination. The black iron gate beckoned and with a touch easily swung open. Her heels clicked across the pink cobblestone walk. She stopped to admire the craftsmanship of the stained-glass door with hues yellows, greens, and purples. It had to be original to the building. The porcelain doorknob was cool in her hand. She twisted it and stepped inside.

A receptionist behind an imposing desk that seemed to take up most of the waiting room, had her attention riveted to the computer monitor.

"Excuse me, I—"

"Do you have an appointment?"

"Yes, with Mr. Abernathy. I'm Denise Sparks."

"He's waiting for you. You're late." She looked up as if demanding an excuse.

"I'm sorry. Traffic, it was, it was, backed up. Past Market Street."

"It's the first office down the hall on the right." The receptionist waved in the general direction and went back to looking at her monitor screen.

Deni snuck a quick glance at the monitor as she walked by. The woman was on Pinterest. No wonder she didn't want to look up from the feast of food splashed across the page. Deni found the office and tapped on the door frame.

Mr. Abernathy bobbed up from behind his laptop. "Denise or rather, Deni. Ann said you preferred that name. Come in, come in. Have a seat."

"I do. It's what my parents called me. The room was empty. Where was the line of chairs filled with people, holding tissues ready to cry? Maybe that only happened in the movies. Instead, two modern-looking chairs stood in front of his desk. She set her purse on the seat of one and slipped onto the other. "I didn't think I was that late. Have the others left already?"

"You are the only one who needed to be here for this part of the will reading. The office was able to administer most of Mrs. Rosen's estate through the mail as it was small." Mr. Abernathy glanced at the papers on his desk. "You may not have known but Mrs. Rosen didn't have any living family and most of her money was used for her care."

"At the nursing home." She tucked her hair behind her ears and leaned forward. "Now I'm even more curious. But, if you mailed everything, what couldn't be mailed?"

"The property at Silverton Lake. I believe you stayed there with her a few summers ago. She left it to you."

"To, to me?" Why didn't she bring tissues? She sniffed. At best she'd hoped for a cookbook or one of her beautiful cross-stitched pillows. Never the house. An image of the comfortable cottage flashed in her mind. The hours she and Ann put together puzzles in the evenings while sipping tea and eating popcorn. And the soft, gentle wind that came off the lake at night, and walking the coastline with Ann. Listening to her reasons why Deni had to learn to trust God's plan even in the dark days.

"However, there are—" Mr. Abernathy's voice interrupted her thoughts. She squirmed in her seat. What had she missed? She looked up. Had he noticed?

"There are a few things that go along with getting the property. Like I said, you must decide if you will accept the conditions of the will within the next twenty-four hours."

"What conditions?" Her stomach jumped.

"You'll need to uproot your life because you must live in the house for three months and move in within the week."

"But..." She gripped the armrests as her stomach contracted in a spasm. Could it be possible God had provided her a way out of the nightmare she now lived? I need to decide and move into the house in seven days?

14

Mr. Abernathy held up his hand. "Before you answer too quickly, there are things to consider. You need to know the house has been vacant for three years. A caretaker was hired to watch over it, but I understand he did minimal upkeep on the house." Mr. Abernathy gathered his papers into a neat pile, clipped them with a paper clip, and set them on the corner of the desk. He settled back and the leather chair protested with a hiss. "Do you understand the stipulations of the will?"

Deni stared out the office window. "The summer my grandmother died, Ann took me and took good care of me. She and my grandmother were best friends. We were both grief-stricken." She swiped a wayward lock of hair away from her eye. "I still don't understand why she would leave the house to me."

"She knew you loved the lake, and more importantly, the house. When we wrote up this will, Ann knew it would be the right place for you to open your business. She mentioned how upset you were when you had to return to the university."

"I planned to stay with her and finish the last semester in Illinois at the local college, but several of my classes wouldn't transfer. I promised to come back to the next summer. Then her hip broke, then pneumonia." Deni paused tasting the saltiness of tears building.

"I visited her at the We Care Center as often as I could. It's so hard to think she's gone." She studied her hands, blinking back hot tears.

"Ann encouraged me to start my stained-glass business. She told me I was wasting my gift from God." Numbness settled over her. "All I have to do is live there for three months?"

"That and sign this." Mr. Abernathy shoved a cream-colored document toward her. "Sign by the X's; here, here, and here." He tapped the lines with his pen before handing it to her.

Deni took the pen and signed. She held the paper for a second. Once Mr. Abernathy took the document her life would change for the better, she hoped. "Here."

"That should do it. You can pick up the keys from Chad Hastings. He owns the boat shop at Wooded Lake. You'll see it before you reach the turn off for Ann's house or rather your house now." He stood and shook her hand. "I hope this works out for you, Deni."

At the door she hesitated, "What happens to the house if I don't stay?"

"Provisions have been made for someone else to take over the property. Are you having second thoughts?" Mr. Abernathy rubbed the back of his neck. "You don't have to accept the house. Better to decide before you uproot your whole life. I'm sure Ann would have understood."

"No. I want to do this. If Ann believed in me that much, then I want to try." She took a breath and blinked back tears. "I won't need the twenty-four hours to decide. I'm going to live my dream."

🐐

Joel Anderson sat in his car and studied his opponent as she left the lawyer's office. This Sparks woman was tiny, but that didn't mean anything in a real estate war. Tiny often meant ferocious, like those little dogs whose demeanor said, "Pick me up." Then they snapped at you. Her floral skirt swished around perfect ankles and caught his eye. Probably a romantic. That's what his sister, Lucy always said. Women who wear flowered clothing are often romantics, who are fond of old books, good movies, cats and lifetime commitments.

The woman's flushed face and her huge smile must mean she'd taken the challenge of living in the house.

Then he saw the circle of white on her neck. Pearls. She wore pearls, like Aunt Bee on that old Andy Griffith show, and he knew, at that moment, this woman would fight him. She would strap on an apron, wear those pearls and embed herself in that house like gold in a mine. Make that a mine two miles underground.

As the Jeep pulled away from the curb, Joel touched the steering wheel to activate his Bluetooth. "Call Chad."

Chad answered before the first ring completed. "Did you get it?"

"Ann left the house to some woman."

"A woman? Why? How could she? Who is she? Do you know her? Do you think she'll sell us the house?" Chad's voice pitched higher with each question.

"I've never met her. I don't know why Ann left her the house. Abernathy say it's hers for the next three months. But if she doesn't stay, then I'm next in line to get the property."

Chad let out a breath. "There's hope then?"

"Maybe she won't stay once she inspects the place. Plus, it's a bit out of town so she might not like being out there alone."

"We have to find a way to make her turn it down."

"Yeah, but if the house doesn't scare her off, I don't think there is much we can do." He recalled the pearls and his shoulders slumped.

"Right."

"We'll have to think of another way to carry out our plan for the resort. We'll discuss it when I get back." He gripped the steering wheel hard. Why did she leave it to this woman? He'd been close to Ann forever. He had hoped the house would go to him. When had she met Ann? And why had Ann never mentioned her?

His dreams would come true with or without the property. He'd spent too much time planning to give up now. A resort would bring in money for the small town. Money needed for a better library and community center. It would bring him more business, too, and that he could handle.

For now, he had another challenge. Stick it out for three months and hope that the pretty Denise Sparks wouldn't stay.

Pretty? Now where had that come from?

🐐

Deni held tight to the steering wheel. Everything had changed. This morning she had a tiny apartment and now a house. A normal morning twisted into a movie script. Wild and amazing.

Was it just her imagination? Or could it be that the summer colors were brighter on the Illinois side of the river? The trees shone in deep shades of jade, the knockout roses in a front yard bright vermilion. The sky itself held a royal tone to it, and a pearly cast dusted the clouds. She wanted to capture this moment in a glass design. Now, thanks to Ann, she would have room to do that.

The garage at the lake house could be made into a comfortable studio. No more trying to work in the tiny second bedroom. Tonight, she would search for the drawing of the sign she once designed. The one she planned to use if she ever opened a studio, but never expected to use. As the excitement of new possibilities surged, goose bumps danced down her arms.

There were many things she had to do and fast. Those three months started as soon as she signed those papers. No need to keep paying rent. Breaking her lease would be the first thing on her list. Not that leaving behind that small, two-bedroom, two-window apartment made her sad. Leaving her part-time cashier position at the hobby store wouldn't bother her, either. And the best thing about this move? She wouldn't have to worry about bumping into her ex-fiancé, Rob, in the teacher's lounge in August.

Telling her friends at church would be hard. And Lori. It would be hard to tell her about this. She wouldn't be happy about Deni moving away. They'd been teaching next to each other for several years. Deni's heart ached. The two of them had been friends since college and getting the call to work in the same school district, the same building, and the same hallway had been something only God could have arranged. Was she throwing away His gift? Or was he giving her another, a bigger slice of life?

This would be a change for the better. She was positive. On the other side of this fear waited an amazing gift. Ann had taught her that.

Never run from fear, but into it.

CHAPTER TWO

Deni drove down the two-lane road, her patience stretched like a piano string. Thankfully with the help of her friends, she managed to pack her apartment before the end of the week. Or at least, managed to get everything in boxes. And who knew what things she would find in them?

Lori promised to make sure the boxes would be labeled with the name of the most important item packed inside. But did Deni's friends consider the same things important?

Lori walked her through canceling the utilities and making arrangements for the electricity and water to be working when she arrived at her new home. She even convinced Deni to get a new phone number. That would keep Rob from calling her or it would until he weaseled someone into giving him her new number. Once he discovered she had a house on a lake, he'd taken an interest in her again. Begging her to take him back.

The Jeep echoed with the nerve-racking howls of her cat.

"Marmalade, kitty, please, hush. You've been shrieking for two hours. We're almost there. Hershey, you'll like having a lake to swim in, and you've been such a good boy. You look like royalty staring out the window. I bet people are saying, Look at that beautiful chocolate Labrador."

On the side of the road, the cornfields rolled past, the lake house seemed farther from St. Louis than she remembered. Each mile took her away from her friends and church. Had she done the right thing?

Her cousin, Terry should arrive at the lake with the small rental truck soon. In her apartment the boxes filled every available inch of the floor but when placed in the truck, they looked lonely stacked in the corner surrounded by empty space.

As she drove, she pictured the herb garden she would plant, full of lavender, thyme, and lemon mint. She visualized the kitchen with gleaming copper pots and shiny counter tops. She could almost inhale the wafting smells of oatmeal raison and cinnamon cookies. A place where children's laughter would bounce from the walls. But it wouldn't be her children.

Passing a sign, she realized that she missed the first entrance to the public boathouse. "Hang on, Hershey!" She made a sharp turn into the gravel drive. She winced at Marmalade's sharp howl. "Sorry, kitty."

She rolled down the windows before getting out and made sure Hershey's leash remained clipped in the doggy seat belt. "I'll be back in a second. Now don't chew the radio knobs, Hershey."

The boat shop sported cobalt blue paint with yellow window trim. Deni picked a penny off the cobblestone sidewalk. "See a penny, pick it up, all day long you'll have good luck." She slid the coin into her skirt pocket, hoping no one saw her childish antics. Not that she cared. Everyone should practice being a child once in a while, and she had the excitement of a first grader on an adventure. The adventure of a new life.

She pushed open the boat shop door. A bell jingled, announcing her arrival.

"I'm out back." The deep male voice floated to Deni from a doorway behind the counter. "Be there in a second."

"Thanks." Deni took a thirty-second tour of the shop. Food supplies, bird seed, motor oil, DVDs, milk, paperback books, and boat parts. Hmm. A quick shop in a boat shop.

"Can I help you?" A man in jeans shorts and a striped shirt stood in the doorway, wiping his oily hands on a rag.

"Mr. Abernathy sent me. I'm looking for Chad Hastings. I'm Deni Sparks."

"I'm Chad. You're the one moving into Ann's place? I sure was surprised to hear she left it to a stranger."

"I wasn't a stranger to her." Her face warmed. "Maybe you weren't here when I lived with her."

"Been here all my life. Must have missed that." Chad turned to a pegboard behind him that held a selection of keys. "You'll need to hire someone to fix all the things that are wrong." He picked up a set with a coral tag. "Here. Glad I don't have to take care of that place anymore." He slid them across the counter. "

"I'm sorry it was such a chore for you," Deni snapped back. She grabbed the and stomped out of the shop.

Back in the Jeep, Deni sped out of the parking lot. "I can't believe the attitude of that guy. He made me feel like I stole the house from Ann."

Hershey yawned, clearly not interested in her troubles.

Deni searched for familiar sites as she drove. She passed a mailbox made to look like a cow. "I remember now. It's just around that corner. It's almost time to get out of your kennel, Marmalade."

She eased the Jeep to a stop next to a mailbox. The once black block numbers resembled more of an artist's sketch now. Queen Anne's lace grew high against the black metal post. The mailbox lid hung like a heavy teardrop from a rusted hinge. Resting inside the box was a bird's nest. "I hope the house is better than this."

When she turned the Jeep down the gravel drive, bubbles built in her stomach, separating and popping. "God, maybe I should have looked at the house before I gave up the apartment. I hope I'm doing what You want me to do."

Gravel crunched under the tires as she drove down the oak tree-lined lane. Abundant weeds intermixed with the limestone rock in the driveway. The back tires plunged into a deep hole and water splashed onto the back window. Marmalade screeched.

Deni came to a jerky stop in front of the house. The front steps rested at an odd angle. A screen hung off a second-floor window. Peeling dove-gray paint clung to the shutters in shreds. In the front garden, a straggly baby's breath and a few daisies weakly stuck their heads out, looking for the sunshine. The gutters exploded with rotten black leaves. Denise moaned. What have I committed myself to?

Hershey whimpered and whacked his tail against the front seat, bringing her back to more pressing needs. "Okay, okay I'll let you out." As soon as she released Hershey's leash, he ran across her lap, not waiting for the door to open completely. Pushing it with his head, he squeezed through the opening and bounded off in the direction of the lake.

"Marmalade looks like you and I get to explore the house together." Denise picked up the kennel and made her way up the wooden steps, careful to avoid the cracks. She wanted to call out to Ann, "I'm here!" Another wave of grief at the loss of her friend ebbed through her.

She put the kennel on the porch, inserted the key and turned, and pushed it open, expecting the door to creak. It didn't.

"Best medicine for sadness is a cuddly kitty." Once inside and with the door closed, she popped the carrier's latch. "Come here, Marmy." She pulled the orange fluff ball from the cage and into her arms. As soon as the purrs started, the ache in her heart eased. Time to look at her new home.

A green and blue braided rug covered part of the light oak living room floor. Across from the fireplace, a blue-striped couch peeked out from under a sheet. A brown leather chair sat near the window, next to a round game table. Filled bookshelves lined one wall. Ornate spider webs decorated a few shelves.

As she walked the short hallway to the kitchen, she hoped her memory matched the reality. When she saw it, she let out a sigh and set Marmalade on the floor. "It's just like I remembered!" She ran her hand against the nearest white cabinet. The glass doors remained intact. A quick cleaning and they would sparkle. Even the blue forget-me-not wallpaper hadn't changed. She closed her eyes for a moment and pictured Ann sitting at the table, sipping tea and reading her Bible.

Hershey barked at the back door. She opened the door and bent down to pet his head. "Good dog." Water dripped off his body, and he wasn't alone.

She rose, noting the tanned, muscled legs. She jerked her head up, acutely conscious of a tall, athletic physique. She met his caramel eyes the same ones that welcomed her to Illinois. A tendril of attraction wound its way through her, a slow flame sprung to life. She glanced away, refusing to acknowledge the feeling. "Hi. I see you've met Hershey."

"You shouldn't let him run loose. Someone might steal him."

"I didn't." She peered up at him. "He smelled the water and took off running. Who are you?"

"I'm Joel Anderson. You're Denise."

"You, you know my name?" She backed away from the door. Was she in danger?

"I apologize. I didn't mean to scare you. When you went into Abernathy's building, it wasn't hard to figure out that you were Denise. Mr. Abernathy told me Ann left the house to you." Joel reached down to scratch Hershey's ears. "When you do decide to leave, the house goes to me."

"You?" He must be the arrangement Mr. Abernathy mentioned.

"I'm next in line. Ann knew I wanted the property, not the house." Joel motioned inside. "Guess she thought you might keep it like it is."

"Don't count on it ever being yours. I'm staying for the next thirty years."

Joel felt as if her green eyes had grown claws ready to rip his skin at the next wrong word. He stood straighter.

Anger turned her cheeks dusty rose. Her wavy hair seemed full of energy. What would that thick hair would feel like in his hands every night for the next thirty years? He brushed off the desire, finally managing to say, "For thirty years?"

Deni smiled, much to his relief. "Maybe not that long, but I do plan to stay. Why do you want this place?"

"I'm an architect. I have plans for the property." Joel captured her gaze. He reached out and caught her hand in his. "Let's start over, please. Hi, I'm Joel Anderson."

Hesitation flitted across her face. She pulled her hand from his.

"Denise Sparks, Deni. Nice to meet you."

"Much better, especially since we are neighbors." Joel glanced back at the Jeep. "Want some help carrying in all those boxes?"

"That's not all of them. The truck will be here later." She flashed a smile. "You're welcome to stick around and help unload it. You know, since we're neighbors and all."

🐐

The door to the moving truck opened. A man dressed in chinos and a checkered shirt stepped out.

Deni stopped short when she noticed what he wore. "Terry, you are going to help unload this thing, aren't you?"

"I suppose I could move a few things for you. I just volunteered to drive the truck remember?" He chuckled.

Behind her, Deni heard Joel coming out of the house. "Joel, I'd like you to meet my cousin, Terry 'Lazybones' Fine."

"That hurts." Terry thrust his hand out to Joel. "I'm really not deserving of that name. She's the one that can trick you into doing her work while she watches." Terry jabbed her in the arm and then winked.

Deni playfully slugged him back.

"I'm kidding, Deni. Open the back and you can get started."

"Like I said, lazy." Deni pushed up the truck door.

"Surprise!"

She squealed as her best friend climbed out of the back. "Lori!"

Hershey barreled around Lori barking in delight.

She dropped to her knees and let Hershey give her doggy kisses. "I've missed you too, buddy."

"Hershey, it's my turn to hug my friend." Deni tugged Lori's freckled arm. "I thought you said you couldn't come."

"Last-minute cancellation meant I was free to help. Terry thought it would be fun to surprise you. That was some bumpy ride down the driveway. And dusty." Lori wiped at a spot on her black Capri pants. "Next time, he can be the surprise."

"I'm so glad you came. I thought it would be weeks before you would get to see my house. Joel, this is Lori. Joel is a neighbor. He volunteered to help me unload the Jeep."

"Volunteered?" Lori's eyebrows arched. "I'm sure that's what happened. Right, Joel?"

"Actually, I think I did."

"Uh huh. When do we get a tour?" Lori asked.

"The place seems to need some work." Terry kicked at a broken shingle lying on the drive.

"Can you believe a caretaker looked after this place?" Deni shook her head. "I guess he didn't know what he was doing—"

Joel's voice stopped her. "My best friend, Chad Hastings, was the caretaker. He did what he could to keep the place standing. Ann didn't pay him or give him any money for repairs. He's a single parent, plus he has the boat shop to run. Doesn't leave him much time to fix things. His main goal was to keep the summer kids from destroying the house."

Deni cringed. "I'm sorry, Joel. I didn't know. I'm afraid that jumping to conclusions is one of my biggest faults. I pray about it often."

Joel stared at her a moment. "I forgive you. If you want to pay someone to help you fix things while you're here, Chad would be good at it."

"What do you meanwhile she's here?" Lori's forehead scrunched. "It's your house, isn't it? You are going to staying, right?"

"Of course, I am. Joel just met me. How could he know how determined I am? He thinks I'll give up and

33

leave this beautiful house. He's hoping because I just discovered that the property then becomes his." Deni frowned at Joel. "You're going to have to realize, I'm not going anywhere."

"It will be nice to have you around the neighborhood for a little while." Joel backed away. "But I'll be surprised if you stay."

Deni shot him with her best teacher-stare, the one that made kids squirm in their chairs. "Come on, everyone. I'll take you on a tour of my house, just as soon as we move the bedroom furniture upstairs."

Terry flexed his muscles. "I'm ready. Joel, if you wouldn't mind, but this will be a lot easier if you help me move that dresser."

"Sure, I'll help with the big stuff."

"Thankfully, my cousin doesn't have a lot of furniture to move." Terry grabbed one end of the dresser. "Just this, a small couch, and the kitchen table."

When they had the furniture inside, they all stood at the back of the moving van. Joel touched Deni's arm. "Hey, all that's left are boxes and I have to run a few errands. I guess I'll see you around." He walked away and then turned. "I want you to know I'll be happy to help you move out when you're ready to leave." He flashed her a grin.

Deni watched him go then turned to Lori. "He couldn't know, could he? I'll never give up this chance God has given me."

"You won't have to. God will work things out. He always does." Lori smiled. "He's cute, you know."

"Who, God? I never thought of Him as being cute, more the kind, grandfatherly type."

"Not God. Joel." Lori glared at her. "You have to learn to love again, Deni. Rob wasn't the right person for you. He was mean-spirited, selfish and a jerk most of the time. You never saw it or chose only to see the best in him. Who knows? Maybe Joel—"

"Jumping caterpillars! Let me move in already and get my business started before you try to marry me off." Deni grabbed a box and stomped up the stairs.

But Lori's words echoed in her mind. Maybe God had given her more than just a chance to make a home and start over.

CHAPTER THREE

Deni waved goodbye one more time as her friends disappeared in a thick gravel dust cloud. With her finger, she snagged the too tight elastic band holding her ponytail and released it. She moved her head in a circle, the cartilage in her neck crackled. She missed her dance class, and the tension from the past few days had found a resting place in her spine.

Hot and sweaty from unloading the truck, she considered a quick dip in the lake. No. Evening would be better.

Inside the kitchen, a stack of boxes waited to be unpacked. A large and lonely task. Her shoulders sagged. It wouldn't be as much fun to unpack as it had been to pack with all her friends around to help.

Hershey nudged her hand, and she rubbed his ear. "Hungry, boy? I'd better feed you and Marmalade before she destroys something."

Deni dug through a box marked in perfect block letters PETS. She tossed crumpled newspaper into the kitchen corner as she removed cans of cat food, a squeaky toy, and a jar of peanut butter. She held the jar, puzzled. Why would that be in the pet box?

At the bottom, she found what she needed. "Tonight you two get to eat from your own bowls. That should make you happy."

She filled Hershey's ceramic bowl to the top with dry dog food. Feeding Marmalade was more difficult. It took emptying several boxes to find the can opener for the shredded tuna. She turned the can over. The gelatinous substance plopped onto the saucer.

"Dinner's ready." She set the bowl down for Hershey and the saucer in front of Marmalade. Marmalade whipped around, flicked her tail in the air, and left the room.

Hershey emptied his bowl, then slid down on the floor, tongue hanging out, and waited close to Marmalade's saucer. He looked at Deni as if to question his right to eat the cat's food.

"Go ahead. She is going to play the picky queen tonight."

Deni's stomach growled. Tired and hungry she continued to rummage through boxes looking for something to eat. It was proving to be a colossal task. She grabbed a soda and a bag of chips her cousin had left. "Hershey, let's go watch the sun set on the beach."

The soft dirt path muffled her footsteps. Over her head the canopy of tree leaves filtered the last of the golden sunlight. Tiny portals of pink and blue peeked through the entwined branches.

The warm earth smell brought back precious memories of a barefoot summer. She stopped and removed her tennis shoes and socks. She set them on the edge of the path.

The picket fence that marked the edge of her property wore its white paint like the hide of an alligator. The gate hinges screeched. "Make a note of that, Hershey. We need to pick up a wire brush and some paint for this fence. Wouldn't hurt to bring oil for those hinges on my next trip to the beach. There might be some of that in the garage. Worth a look and that's a fast and easy fix."

The coolness of the stone steps worn smooth from many years of weather caressed the soles of her feet. Driftwood, dried leaves, and woody rose bushes filled both sides of the steps. She sat on the last step and hugged her knees to her chest.

"This is going to take forever to clean up. Father, are you sure this is where you want me? I'm not a gardener, but I've wanted to learn. Is this going to be another way of yours to teach me patience?"

Hershey licked Deni's chin. She stood. "I'm coming, boy. I said we were going to the lake, and we are. I just needed a moment with my Father."

Hershey ran past her, straight into the water and captured a floating stick.

Deni took small steps to the water's edge and then rolled up her pants legs.

Edging closer she tickled the top of the water with her toes. She shrieked. She expected it to hold the warmth of late summer. Her mistake. It took time to heat this much water. In another month, it would be perfect.

She strolled along the water's edge until her toes numbed. A heart-shaped rock caught her attention. She stooped to pick it up and slid it into her pocket to add to her collection.

Deni sat on the beach, watching Hershey run in the shallow water, biting at the tiny waves. "It can't get any better can it, Lord?" Deni lay back to watch the sunset. Vivid orange, yellow, and red ran and dripped together like a child's watercolor painting.

A sailboat's blue and white canvas tripped up and over the small waves. Peace filled her heart.

Footsteps crunched on the rocks behind her. She turned to look. It was Joel bearing a blanket and a wicker picnic basket. Lori was right. He was cute. That blue and white striped T-shirt showed off his well-formed chest. She had to be careful of thoughts like that.

Remember the list.

She wrote it when she was sixteen and placed it in her grandmother's jewelry box. Time to get it out and read it again. This time, the man she dated would meet every item on that list before she got serious about anyone ever again.

🐐

Joel stopped at Deni's feet. "Hi, neighbor. I brought dinner because it's hard to find the energy to get a decent dinner together the first night in a new home. I hope you don't mind cold sandwiches."

"Thank you, but how did you know that my friends weren't staying?"

"Lori made it clear they had to return the truck before dinnertime. I think she was hinting you would be here all alone without any food or human company."

He watched the warmth inch up her cheeks. It enhanced her beauty. Did she know that?

"I'm sorry. Sometimes, Lori can be a mother hen."

"No worries. I need to eat, and I don't mind having company during a meal."

"That's odd. I thought you wanted me to leave. Seems strange for you to show up with a welcome meal." She pursed her lips.

Joel shrugged. "You're right, but I thought it wouldn't hurt to be nice. Make no mistake. I do want the house. Ann must have considered you wouldn't since she made it clear you had to live here for three months. I can wait. Once you give up, I'll get on with my plans. "

"I like an honest man. At least, I know what you want from me."

Joel looked away. Did she realize what she'd said could be taken another way? He hoped not. Hershey splashed along the shoreline. "He likes the water, doesn't he?"

"Too much. When he was a puppy, I had to keep the bathroom door shut, or he jumped in the bathtub with me. There just isn't enough room in most tubs to hold a Labrador and a person, nor did I wish to share. That's why I'm so happy to be here. Labs have energy off any scale I've ever seen. My apartment was small, so Hershey and I did many laps around the block."

"Why did you buy him? Didn't you know you needed a bigger place for him?"

"I did. God knew Hersh needed a home and fast. I went to the humane society for a small dog, maybe a terrier. Instead, there was Hershey. He was scheduled to lose his life that night. I couldn't let that happen."

"He's a beautiful dog. Why would someone put him in the pound?"

"The card attached to his cage said he destroyed furniture." Deni laughed. "I didn't have much furniture, so I wasn't worried about him damaging anything. I bought a kennel and put him inside when I had to leave. He learned to chew only his toys and maybe a shoe or two of mine."

"And now he's here, with a lake for entertainment."

"God knew Hersh, and I needed to move, and He provided us with more than I could have imagined. Would you like to eat here or at my new home?"

"Here is fine." Joel tossed the blanket to Deni, and she caught it. Together, they spread it out, placing the basket in the middle between them.

"Would you like to say grace?"

"No. I'll let you since I brought the meal."

She cocked her head and gave him a look he couldn't interpret. "Fold your hands, then."

After her short prayer, Joel handed her a turkey sandwich and a soft drink. "What kind of business do you have?"

"I work with stained glass. It's a small business right now. I have a few clients, but now, thanks to Ann, I have the freedom to pursue it as a career."

"How did you get started doing that?" Joel dug into the potato chip bag.

"When I was little, we went to a church that had stained glass windows. I loved the way the light streamed in from the sun. All those magnificent colors. Then one Sunday, I wanted to make stained glass for my bedroom window. I spent hours coloring on white tissue paper. I cut it into hundreds of pieces and then glued them on."

"What was the picture?"

"A white stallion with an emerald eye. I poked a hole in the eyepiece to let the sun shoot through. So many tiny bits and pieces of paper. It must have taken me hours to make it."

"Why a white horse?"

She shrugged. "I'm not sure. I might have tired of coloring all those small pieces. I remember I had the horse standing on a mountain with wildflowers."

"Very industrious. How old were you?"

"Ten. I've been told I disappeared into my room and didn't come out until I was called for suppertime. That's when my parents discovered the window." Deni frowned. "I also spent hours scraping the glue off the window."

Joel laughed. "So at ten years old, you knew you wanted to make stained glass windows?"

"It took longer than that. I always loved to go to downtown St. Louis and look at the stained windows in the old brick houses. When I was in high school I decided to take a class to see if I could make them. I liked it so much took lessons at a studio in Clayton."

"You've been in business since high school?" Joel finished his meal and stretched his legs to the side of the blanket.

"I've have worked with glass since then, but I haven't been in business that long. I didn't think I could support myself that way. Instead I went to college and became a teacher."

"Is something wrong? You look sad."

"No, not really. I'm just going to miss the kids and their funny stories." Deni smiled. "So, what odd thing did you do as a child?"

"I'm trying to remember if I did something that predicted my future as an architect." Joel put his hand to his forehead. "Let me think."

Deni wrapped her arms around her knees and wiggled her toes. "It shouldn't be this hard."

"Got it. When I was eleven, I built a castle using marshmallows and peanut butter."

"Did you make a moat, too?"

"Nope, I didn't get to. My mom discovered me holding a knife loaded with peanut butter, and that was the end of the castle keep."

"What happened?"

"She made me throw it away. She said it would attract bugs. Then with my allowance I had to buy another bag of marshmallows. They were supposed to be for my sister, Lucy to take to her Girl Scout campfire."

"That's was only fair, but didn't your mom want to encourage your creativity?"

"Maybe if I hadn't been building on her prized cherry wood sideboard." Joel grinned. "I tried to explain the allure of the supplies lying there, waiting for my creative genius, and that I didn't even eat any of them, but she didn't buy it."

Hershey ran toward them with a stick in his mouth. Deni jumped up, raised her hand in the air, palm out. "Stay."

Hershey skidded to a stop at the edge of the tablecloth, then dropped the stick at Joel's feet and shook. Beads of water sprayed everywhere.

Laughing, Joel wiped water off his face. "Guess that's the end of dinner."

"Sorry." Deni stacked the plates in the wicker basket. She handed the basket to Joel. "I need to go back and unpack a few things before tomorrow. Thanks for bringing dinner."

"Would you like some help? I mean, do you need to move any boxes somewhere? No unpacking, though. I don't like to empty boxes and stand around trying to find a place to put things."

"No, I don't need any help. I can do it myself." She called Hershey and headed up the steps without looking back at him.

Independent, with a touch of bravado. Yes, she was here to stay.

🐐

Deni tried to lift a heavy carton of photo albums from the bedroom floor. Somehow, they had ended upstairs, and she wanted them on the bookshelf downstairs. She shoved and scooted the box toward the door and regretted not accepting Joel's offer. His muscles would have would have been helpful. In his hands, the box would be as light as marshmallows.

She would have to ask for help, and she hated that. Maybe she could step over it tonight. Leave them until Lori came for a visit? The last thing she needed was to be thinking of Joel and the warmth of his hand in hers. And how she didn't want to let go. She must learn to depend on herself. That must be another reason she was here, far from friends, and without the man she thought loved her.

"Enough of that pity party. Hershey, it's time for bed." He hopped up to his rightful place on the bed. He grabbed a pillow, shook it, and then tossed it on the floor.

At least, his actions were typical. He didn't seem to be sad about leaving the apartment. But then, she'd moved him to the best place on earth. With her and a lake in the back yard. Tomorrow she'd unload the box an album or two at a time and take them downstairs. Problem solved. After that many trips, her leg would ache, but it would be better than having Joel in her bedroom.

CHAPTER FOUR

Joel rode shotgun in Chad's truck. They finished their routine Sunday breakfast at his house. Having Chad's son, Doug, help crack eggs always made him wish he had his own kid. After eating, they thought it would be a good time to see what kind of work Deni might hire Chad to do.

Chad stopped his rusted pick up close to Deni's back door. He turned the ignition key. It took a few minutes for the engine to quiet.

"Dad says the horses aren't ready to stop running yet. Joel, do you think there are real horses in the engine?"

Joel rubbed Doug's chin with his thumb. "You bet. When you start driving, you'll find them too. You can't see them until you get your driver's license."

"Too soon to talk about that, Joel." Chad unbuckled his son's seat belt. "Doug is thinking about a bigger bike."

"Dad, when can I get mine? Noah has one already."

"See what you've started, Joel?"

"The boy just wants to be like his friends." Joel climbed out of the truck. "I don't see her Jeep. Maybe she parked in the garage."

"Doug and I'll wait here." Chad leaned against the front of the truck, patting the hood for Doug to stand next to him.

Joel knocked on the back door. The windowpane shook, moving the curtains. "Need to fix this window. The pane is loose," he yelled to Chad.

Hershey launched into a barking frenzy.

Joel peeked through the widow. He spied boxes spread out across the floor, some of them open. How much unpacking had Deni managed the night before? From the looks of the kitchen, she didn't get far.

Joel walked back to the truck. "She must not be home. She may not have heard me knocking, but the dog would have alerted her. Let's hang around for a bit."

"We should leave and come back later." Chad shifted his weight back and forth glancing down the drive, then at his son. Doug pulled a small car from his jeans pocket and dropped to his knees on the driveway. He drove on a make-believe road.

"Gotta push those horses. Brrummm." Doug's lips vibrated with engine noises.

"We'll go in a minute. Just walk around and try to get an idea of what you want to charge her to fix it up." Joel viewed the weed growth. It hurt to see them. Ann always had an array of flowers planted, different ones every year. She said she liked to announce a new spring with a new rainbow of colors. He could still see her dressed in her pink-and-white-striped apron to protect her clothes while she worked. Often, he found her in the garden weeding and collecting flowers in an old, funny-shaped basket. Maybe he should save the house.

"I wonder if Deni will replant this garden, bring it back to what it used to be?"

Chad glared at Joel. "I don't get it. I thought you wanted her to leave, and now you're talking flowers? Why do you want me to fix up the place? It'll make it harder to get her out if everything works."

"I was thinking about revamping my plan. This place could make a nice rental cottage or an office so we might as well help her get it into shape. Maybe once she realizes how difficult it is to live alone and there's so much to maintain here." Joel hesitated. "Maybe, if there's too much work, too much money involved...she'll go..."

"She'll head back to where she belongs." Chad nodded toward Doug and motioned to Joel to walk over to the house. "I see where you're going. The plan is to charge a lot and take my time getting the work done."

"No. Just be fair. I don't want to get the house dishonestly. Maybe she won't like living out here alone after a few weeks."

"Looks like she's going to need new shutters. It would take a lot of work to redo them." Chad backed up to inspect the shingles. "Could use a new roof, too."

Joel sat on the porch steps. "Do you remember when we were kids? How we'd sit here dreaming about how cool it would be to have a resort here in Silverton and how we would build it."

"Sure, you were going to design it and a boat dock. I was going to build it." Chad frowned. "The dock was going to be mine. I planned to rent slips to boat owners by the month. Maybe get a few speed boats and skis to rent to the resort." Chad narrowed his eyes. "I thought we were going to get to do it this time."

Joel watched Doug play in the dirt, remembering two small boys and promises made to each other long ago. "We still can If she leaves. We won't open this summer, but we can start work in August." He squinted, trying to peer through the thickened trees. "We used to be able to see the lake from these steps."

Chad ground the dirt with his foot. "We will again," he mumbled. "If I have anything to do with it."

"What?"

"Nothing. Come on, Doug, let's check the back of the house."

In the fellowship hall, Deni stood surrounded by some of her friends from the Wednesday night Bible study group. She glanced around, trying to spot Lori. She needed her friend to rescue her soon to keep the tears from falling. How did she ever think she could leave this church family, especially this group? They had been by her side with prayers, food and even walks with Hershey when Rob broke off their engagement.

"Do you think you could come back once in a while for a meeting, Deni?" Kelly asked her, tears in her eyes.

"No. I'd like to, but it's such a long drive, and at night it would seem farther. Don't you dare cry, Kelly. If you start, then I'll be crying with you."

"Right. This is supposed to be a happy time for her," said Alex, Kelly's husband, as he put his arm around Deni. "She gets to follow her dream. Until the next time."

"Alex, you're right. I will be back — just not every week."

"Hug time?" Lori asked. "I've been trying to get over here to talk to you, Deni, but I had so much fun in the nursery this morning I had trouble leaving the kids when the Sunday school shift arrived."

"Alex and Kelly are trying to make me feel better about leaving."

"I think this would be a good time to take off, now that Lori is here." Kelly said.

Deni gave the pair another quick hug. "Thank you both, and whatever you do, don't quit praying for me. Maybe at the end of the summer I can have you out for a barbecue."

"Sounds good, I'll volunteer to grill if you like." Alex winked. "Unless by then there is another male around who has become territorial by then."

"Not likely. Please, consider the job yours." Deni watched them walk away. Alex stopped and wiped a tear from Kelly's cheek and then leaned over to say something into her ear that made her stand taller. Someday she hoped to have an Alex in her life, though with every male she dated the possibility seemed to shrink.

"Deni, are you leaving now, or do you have time to go to lunch and talk?" Lori smiled. "Maybe you have something to tell me about last night?"

"Oh that, nothing much. Joel asked me if I would please be the mother of his children." Deni turned and headed for the door. Maybe she could make it to her Jeep before every detail of the evening was extracted from her. Sometimes her friend could be a bit invasive into Deni's life.

"What?" Lori caught up with her. "Stop. You can't leave me with that announcement. I need details."

"Got you. That's what you get for sending him out with a picnic dinner as if I couldn't possibly feed myself."

"How romantic. Where were you at your house or the beach?"

"The beach, and that is all I'm going to tell you." Deni smiled. "At least for now." She opened the Jeep door, letting the built-up heat escape before attempting to climb inside.

"There's more? You have to tell me. I don't do chapter installments with grace. You know that. Please, tell me." Lori leaned against the Jeep and pleaded with a sad face.

She softened. Her friend only wanted Deni to be happy. "It was a nice dinner. We talked about how we chose our professions and then I went home. See there wasn't much more to tell you."

"Just wait, maybe there will be more soon. You never know what God has planned, do you?"

"No, but I can see you planning how to get us together, Lori and I don't think that is what He meant about being His instrument." Deni put on her sternest face. "Leave it alone. I'm fine the way my life is now."

Lori grinned. "Understood. But if you aren't interested in Joel would you mind if I became interested?"

Shaken by her question, Deni searched for a response. "I...I hadn't, I guess it would..."

"Stop!" Lori laughed. "No, you aren't interested, are you? It was a test, and you flunked."

"Maybe I'll give him a chance. It's not likely that he'll manage to meet the list requirements, though."

"That list has to go. It's just a protection device to keep you out of relationships."

"Maybe it is, but it's what I need to do."

🐐

Deni pulled her Jeep next to an unfamiliar brown pickup. Hershey didn't like the company from the sound of his barking when she opened the Jeep door. Careful not to catch her long skirt, she slid it off the seat before slamming the door. Joel, and the man from the boat shop, Chad, stood in the yard staring up at her roof. And whose little boy was that?

"Hi, Joel. What are you doing here?"

"Last night, you mentioned the possibility of hiring Chad to do some of the work that needs to be done, so I thought I'd bring him over and reintroduce you." Joel scratched his chin. "Does this happen to you a lot, having to be reintroduced to people?"

"No. Never. Hi Chad. Can you help get the house back the way it should be."

Chad folded his arms across his chest. "I'd be interested. I'll have to come by in the evenings. That's the only time I'm available. I'll have to bring my son along, too. Doug, get up and say hi to Miss-?"

"Sparks. Hi, Doug. How old are you?"

"Five. Can I play with your dog?"

"Yes, you can. Hershey likes little boys and so do I. What is your favorite kind of cookie?"

"Chocolate chip. But I eat the chips out of the bag if there aren't any cookies. Dad said it's just as good as eating a real cookie."

"Then I'll make sure I have real cookies and have a bag of chocolate chips to eat when you come to help your dad."

"Okay."

Chad looked over his shoulder at Joel. "How much longer is this going to take? I need to get Doug to his grandmother's."

Maybe this wasn't a good idea. "If you don't want to do this, I'm sure I can find someone else."

"No, I don't mind. I can use the extra cash."

"Good, I'm glad." Deni flashed him a grin hoping to get one in return. "Why don't you take your son? I'll make up a list of what needs to be done. In fact, I've already started it. Then maybe you could drop by later, and we'll go over it."

"It'll take about an hour. See you, Joel, Deni. Doug, time to go to your grandmother's." Once they were in the truck, Chad slammed his door. The engine sputtered, then caught, sending black smoke from the tailpipe.

Deni waited until Chad drove off before turning to Joel. "I thought you said he was nice. You say he's your best friend?" She struggled not to add more.

"He's had a rough time since his wife, Mandy, died. He'll come around. Give him some time."

Deni hesitated. "How did she die?"

"Cancer, about six months ago. Since then, Chad's been working at the boathouse for his father."

"I'm sorry. I hope the pain eases soon for him. What did he do before he started working for his father?"

"He was a general contractor. He lost his business not long after Mandy was diagnosed. He never finished any jobs. Couldn't. He stayed home to help her." Joel motioned to the door. "Aren't you going to let the dog out?"

Deni fumbled for the key chain she had stuck in her skirt pocket. She pulled it out along with the church bulletin. The keys fell to the ground.

Joel reached down to pick them up. He read the inscription on the silver heart, ...a time to dance, Ecc. 3:4. What does that mean?"

"It's personal." She reached for the key ring. As Joel handed it back to her, his hand covered hers, and he trailed his fingers over her outstretched palm.

Deni jerked away as if it had touched a hot wire. "Thanks." Flustered by her reaction, she rammed the key into the lock. "I need to let

Hershey out before he tears through the door." Twisting the knob with one hand and the key with the other, she managed to release him.

Hershey pushed past Deni and took off toward the lake.

She yanked the key from the lock and held it up to show Joel its bent shape. "I think I need to add new locks to the list. It's getting longer. I just hope I have enough money to get all the work finished."

"Guess you could always go back to St. Louis and teach if you run out of money. You might not like living here in the winter, anyway. When it snows, sometimes you can't get to town for days."

"I have a Jeep, remember? Don't worry about me. I'll know that I'll love it here even with snow and ice." She went inside and slammed the door. For a man who was considerate enough to treat her to dinner on her first night in a strange place, he was awful intent on seeing her leave

CHAPTER FIVE

Crumpled notebook paper crowded one corner of Deni's tiny desk. A teacup boasting bright red and yellow flowers perched on its matching saucer. A small plate sprinkled with toast crumbs rested nearby. Deni leaned back in the ladder-back chair and raked her fingers through her hair. With a sigh, she reached for the letter she had just finished writing. She read it, then grabbed the top of the paper and ripped it from the notebook. Scrunching the loose paper into a ball, she tossed it on top of the growing pile of discarded letters. Frustrated, she tried again.

"Dear Mr. Townsend, I regret that I must return my teaching contract unsigned." She tapped her ink pen on the desktop and looked out the window. A small breeze rifled the top of the trees. The flower bed still overflowed with weeds. The gravel she ordered for the driveway still hadn't been delivered. And she still hadn't made a decision.

Stay or leave. Go back to the familiar or take the challenge of being in business on her own. Enjoy the excitement of working with leaded glass or be frightened of being the boss.

She had avoided seesaws after the first time she'd been coaxed onto one by a friend. Memories rushed through her mind, sent her heartbeat soaring. Up and down. Until Mike jumped off, leaving her unbalanced, and sent her crashing to the ground, terrified. Now, she sat on a seesaw, waiting to be dropped again. Only this time it would be worse than breaking an arm.

Sending the contract back unsigned meant she would have to give up her steady income. The full trust fund her parents set up for her wouldn't be available for another year. Unless she used the Guilt Fund awarded to her. It was meant to replace her parents after the plane crash. No. She'd take the worst job she could imagine before using one cent.

Deni picked up her Bible and searched for Proverbs 3:5-6. "Trust in the Lord with all your heart and lean not on your own understanding; in all your ways acknowledge him and he will make your paths straight."

She closed the book and set it on the desktop. She waited savoring the words. Then, she picked up her pen and finished the letter.

God has presented me with an opportunity to follow my dream. I have always taught my students to follow their hearts. I feel at this time that I must take my own advice. I am returning my contract to you, unsigned.

She folded the letter in thirds and stuffed it with the contract in an envelope. Holding it in her hand, she couldn't bring herself to seal it. The toast sat like lead balls in her stomach. Deni allowed one more moment of regret. She wouldn't walk into a classroom this fall. There wouldn't be a freshly cleaned white board or the nervous smiles of new students. She wouldn't see any of the students she had taught last year and worse yet, she might never know how they were doing in the sixth grade.

Stop it. If I really want to see them, I can. I can drive back for a visit. Maybe I can even do a workshop with the kids, using colored plastic instead of glass. With a leap of faith, she sealed the envelope and stamped it. She had officially cut all ties. Now all that was left to do was make her business grow enough to support herself. She wouldn't ask for more than that. The possibilities were endless and daunting. She would be entirely on her own.

🐕

Deni's jeans were wet and bleached splattered. Her knees went numb from kneeling on the kitchen floor. She held a toothbrush in her right hand and a spray bottle of bleach in her left. She sprayed the grimy grout between the light-blue ceramic tiles. She gazed at the expanse of floor tiles and groaned. Her back ached. "I'm not even halfway through yet."

At the quiet knock on the screen door, Deni looked up, surprised to see Chad and Doug. She stood, walked to the door, and opened it wide.

"Hi, Chad. Doug. Are you here to work?" Deni waited for Chad to say he was quitting or that he wanted more money. To her surprise, he smiled.

"Morning. I had some time and figured I'd work on those shutters since you don't want to replace them. Nail them back onto the house. Then they won't bang on the house in the wind. Doug is going to help me. If that's okay?" Chad held a brown paper bag.

"That would be great. No more banging in the wind." She pointed at the bag. "Do I owe you for nails or something?"

"No. This is our lunch. Could I put it in your fridge?"

"We're having peanut butter on crackers and chips." Doug piped in. "We have sodas, too."

Laughing at the boy's excitement, Deni took their lunch from Chad. "It'll be here when you're ready for it." She glanced at the wet floor; never mind that she would have to walk across it to get to the fridge. It wasn't worth mentioning. Not when Chad's attitude had changed toward her. He even whistled as he walked away from the house. Maybe she had been wrong about him.

For the last time, Deni stood, stretched, and tossed the rag and toothbrush into the bucket. The grout shone bright white. "That is a job I hope I never have to repeat before I die, Hershey."

Stiff-legged, she climbed over the stacked boxes in the doorway that kept Hershey off the wet floor.

He licked her hand and barked at her as if they'd been separated by miles.

"All right boy, we'll get the mail."

Hershey spun in circles and pranced about the room as she took the leash from the front doorknob.

"Sit, or I won't get this on you. We aren't going on a mile-long walk, goose. Just to the end of the drive. Now, sit."

Hershey sat. His front legs slid on the wooden floor until he laid flat. Deni hooked the leash to his collar, and he sprang up, pulling Deni toward the door.

She didn't see Chad or Doug anywhere. Maybe they were taking a break on the beach. The ladder was still propped against the house, so Chad hadn't finished. She stepped back to see what he had done. Four of the shutters now hung straight and sturdy.

Hershey tugged on the leash.

"I know, you either want to walk or be free. Mailbox first, buddy. I don't want you to forget what it's like to be tethered to me."

The changing leaf shadows made patterns on the driveway and reminded her of a fairy tale land. "Ah, if only there were a real prince on his way to find me. One who meets everything on my list. What do you think, Hershey? Is there one out there for me?"

A squirrel scurried across the driveway in front of them. Hershey strained on his leash and yanked Deni toward the woods.

"Hershey, heel." She snapped the leash hard.

He slowed until he pranced next to Deni.

"Good boy." Deni patted him on the head. "No squirrel chasing today. It's too hot."

At the mailbox, Deni flipped through the assorted 'dear occupant' mail offering cleaning services and coupon for a dentist. A horn beeped. "Hershey, heel!"

Joel slowed his car to a stop in front of her and lowered his window. Her heart raced like a junior high girl seeing her boyfriend at her locker between classes. Stop! Remember, he thinks you'll be gone in three months. No long-term commitment awaits with him.

Hershey barked. His tail wagged hard enough to shake his body.

"He's happy to see me."

"You can think you're special if you like, but he treats all his friends that way."

"Did you get everything unpacked?"

"Most of the boxes are empty. I'm still trying to find things, though. I seem to have unpacked things in odd places. I found the catsup bottle in the linen closet yesterday."

"I imagine you'll probably find several things in the wrong place for a while." Joel fingertips drummed the side of the car. "Maybe you would like to go to dinner."

"That would be heaven. I've been on the kitchen floor all morning scrubbing the grout, and I didn't relish the idea of making dinner." Deni wrinkled her nose. "I was planning on a bagel or a can of spaghetti."

"Then come to my place tonight. My mom keeps me supplied with lasagna."

The cool wind rushing from the car window couldn't extinguish the flame burning her face. "There goes my impulsiveness again. I'm sorry. I thought you were asking about tonight."

"It's not a problem. I can thaw and reheat like a pro. Besides, if you come to my house, I can show you the model of the resort that I've put together."

Deni pulled herself up to her full height of five foot three inches. "Joel—"

"Hold on! I just want to show you what I had planned for when you leave. If you leave."

"I told you, I'm staying. But I would like to see your idea for when you find a different property for sale. What time should I be there?" She reeked of bleach. "I hope not too soon. I need to do some major cleaning up."

"About six?" Joel leaned out the window to pet Hershey. "Bring him if you want."

"How do I get to your house?" Deni looked down the long stretch of asphalt.

"Why don't you walk the beach? Hang a right at the water's edge. You can't miss it. I'm your neighbor. Shouldn't take more than ten minutes."

"Should I bring something?"

"Dessert?" He gave her a little boy smile.

Her breath caught. Could he get any cuter? "I think I can rustle up something."

His smile went from a little boy to a male model. "I can't wait. See ya."

Joel's black sports car sped off and disappeared around the corner. "Hershey, would Joel qualify as a prince for saving me from cooking tonight? He does look like one. But his car is the wrong color for a modern-day prince. It should be silver or white, not black. And he doesn't want to rescue me." She kicked a piece of gravel.

CHAPTER SIX

Deni arrived at Joel's house as the sun hung low in the sky, streaked in shades of fuchsia, scarlet, and variegated blues. The cake basket in her hand swung from its handle.

A cupola cast a soft ivory light over the gray-blue shingles. Did Joel go up there often and watch the sunset? Or was he a sunrise guy? Three white steps led to three French doors. Two windows topped each door, and a triangle-shaped window crowned the entire thing. She spied honey oak walls glowing through the glass. For a second, it felt like home. Then Joel came to the door. Framed in the light and glass, she was acutely aware of the strength in his muscled arms and core. He'd be able to twirl her over his head with ease. She almost laughed. He probably found designing buildings more appealing than ballet.

"Right on time." Joel took the basket from her and led her inside. "What kind of cake?" He lifted the basket to his nose and sniffed.

"Angel food. You must not get dessert often."

"Can't bake at all. Dinner is just about ready to come out of the oven. You didn't bring Hershey?"

"No, I knew he'd play in the lake on the way and he'd be a mess." She followed him into the kitchen. It exuded the warmth of an old country kitchen, right down to a rocking chair in the corner. "Did you design your house?"

"Sort of. I found two barns that I liked, had them dismantled and then put them together in a different way." He pulled the lasagna out of the oven. "I have the before and after pictures if you want to see them, after dinner."

"Were they real barns? With stalls?"

"Yes, complete with milking stations, troughs for the pigs and a hayloft."

"You are good at what you do."

"Thanks. Would you grab the salad out of the fridge? And then follow me." Joel led the way to the dining room.

The dining room had two of the walls of glass. One had a beautiful view of the lake, the other a corner of the woods. Tiny ships inserted into glass bottles lined shelves along one interior wall. She set the salad on the table and picked up one of the bottles. "I've always wondered how they get those boats through that tiny opening."

"Someday, I'll show you. My grandfather made most of those." Joel poured ice water from an odd-shaped green ceramic pitcher.

"Where did you get this?" She ran her hand over the bumpy surface. "It reminds me of a pickle."

"Local artist at the high school. They had a show, and this one looked so..."

"Unique?"

"Yes, the student artist wore such a pained expression. Pretty sure she didn't want to be there. I've been told it's a requirement for the freshman art class to participate in a show."

At the table, Deni waited, hands folded in her lap.

"Would you like me to say grace?"

Her heart beat fast just for a second, remembering the first item on her date list, then she nodded. "Please."

Joel bowed his head. Deni watched him for a moment. Then did the same as he began. "Father, thank You for this meal You alone have provided. Thank You for new friendships. In Jesus' name. Amen."

"Amen." His words touched her. Maybe—

"Oops." He sprang up from his seat, scattering her thoughts like spilled seeds.

"The bread! I left it in the oven." He bolted to the kitchen then came back carrying a basket of rolls, his right arm draped with a white dishcloth. "Would you care for one?"

"Are you always this proper?"

"I've had excellent training, my grams was insistent that I learn my manners. It started with my sister bugging me and Grams took offence. Thankfully I only have one sister. Who knows what would have happened if I'd managed to disrespect a bunch of them." Joel sat in his chair. "How about you? Brothers and sisters?"

"No siblings. No. I wish but my parents were killed in an airplane crash. I was brought up by my grandmother." Deni recited in a singsong voice.

"Sounds like you've had to say that a lot." His wore the pity face she knew all too well.

Deni shrugged. "I have. I was six when they crashed. One hundred and thirteen people were killed." Joel put his fork down and touched her hand. "I'm sorry. That must have been a frightening time for you. Where were they going?"

"My dad had a business trip. Grandmother said Dad talked Mom into going with him." Ready to change the subject, Deni picked up her plate and glass. "I'll put these in the kitchen."

Joel followed her with his dishes. "Set these on the counter and I'll do them later. Want to see my resort now?"

"Sure, I'd like to see what you think would look better than my little house." Deni folded her arms against her chest.

Joel led the way to his office. A spotlight shone on a small desk that held a model constructed of small plastic bricks. The model sat on a board covered with tiny trees and blue paint for the lake. There was even a minuscule sailboat anchored by the island.

"A Victorian house. I've always wanted to live in one of those. I wanted an attic to play in when I was little."

"You sound so wistful."

"Um. I am. I always wanted a home of my own with lots of kids someday. This is the house of my dreams."

"So you understand why I want your property?"

She turned and looked at him. "Maybe something else will come up for sale."

"I'm short on funds to buy another place. If you leave the house, I won't have to buy it." Joel's face resembled cold marble.

Chills scratched her spine. "It's getting late. I think it's time to go. We've been over this argument. I'm not leaving my cottage. Thank you for dinner." Deni strode through the house.

"Wait, let me walk you home." He touched her elbow. "You didn't bring a flashlight."

She stopped. If she walked the beach in the dark, she might trip over driftwood. She could hurt herself and lie there for hours. "I didn't leave a light on at the house either." She sighed in defeat.

They strolled along the beach, not speaking. Only the lapping water made a sound in the night as it slapped the shoreline. A half-moon shone from its lofty perch, its beams dancing on the water's edge. Joel smelled good. There, she'd admitted it, at least to herself. He smelled better than good. She edged a little closer.

"Look, there's a boat by the island." Joel surprised her by resting his arm on her shoulders and turning her toward the water. "I love to watch the boats, even at night with their blinking red and green lights. It's harder to tell how big they are, or if they are fishing boats, or just out for a pleasure ride."

She relaxed against his shoulder and tried to concentrate on the boat. "What do you suppose they're doing?"

"I imagine those are pirates, waiting for some unlucky ship to cross their path."

Deni laughed. "I think it's a mom and pop. The kids have moved out, and they are searching for a romantic moment."

"Nope, pirates. Has to be pirates. More fun that way."

Deni pulled away from Joel. Nope, not the man on the list. Not if he couldn't imagine a romantic scene.

But if he didn't want her around, why did this feel like a date?

🐐

At Deni's house, lights from every window split the darkness into many layered shadows. "I didn't think I left the lights on."

"Are you sure?"

"It's probably nothing. Maybe I did. Sometimes I get distracted."

"Enough to leave on all the lights?"

Deni shook her head no.

"I'm checking out the house. I want to make sure you're safe."

"You don't need to. I'll be fine." She stepped into the kitchen and stopped.

Joel bumped into her.

"Snakes!" Three snakes wiggled in different directions across the newly cleaned kitchen floor. Her stomach rolled. Joel's hand, massive and strong, spun her out of the way.

He reached out and caught the closest one. "They're just black snakes; they won't hurt you. You want this kind around but not in your house. I'll catch them and put them outside. Why don't you wait on the porch?"

Deni stumbled to the front porch. She leaned against the peeling banister. *Father, is this a sign from you? Am I making the wrong decision about staying here?*

Joel and Hershey came around the front. "I let him out of the bathroom."

"The bathroom? I didn't put him in there. That's odd. Are the snakes gone?" She shivered at the thought of them slithering across her floor.

"Yes, they're gone." Joel stared at her. "Look, you don't belong in this old place. Why don't you let me take it? I can make you a stockholder in the resort. That will give you some money, eventually."

"No. I can't leave. I sent back my teaching contract unsigned. I have nowhere to go, nowhere to live." She trembled thinking about starting over again, going back to where she would see Rob every day. Her dream dead, no longer a possibility.

"Are you cold?" Joel pulled her into his embrace. "You look like my little sister Lucy when she's scared, all wide-eyed like a deer, with goose bumps. She says a hug always helps."

Deni sunk into his warm chest. The tension melted away. He smelled like soft leather, warm hay, and sunshine. Her fear dissolved replaced by comfort. "Lucy is right. Thanks for coming to my rescue, Joel." She stepped away

"Playing on my soft side? No place to go, huh? You've closed every door and burned the bridge?" He caressed her cheek.

Deni barely tilted her lips into a smile. "It's true. I don't have any place of my own to run to. That's why I want this house. I want to open that back door and know it's mine, that I belong here."

Joel rested his hand on her shoulder. "I think I understand. Have Chad check tomorrow to see if he can figure out how the snakes got inside. I looked through the house. Nothing seems to be disturbed. It's odd that all the lights were on. And that the dog was in the bathroom. Someone may have broken in. We can call the police if you want."

"No. What would I report? You said there wasn't anything wrong inside. And Hershey often locks himself in rooms by banging against the door with his big head. And maybe I did leave the lights on. It's a new place to me and I may have thought I turned them off when I left." Deni stood on the porch steps, not quite ready to enter the house alone. "Would you like to come in for a while?"

"Maybe next time. I've some work to finish." Joel brushed past her and then turned at the bottom of the stairs. "Will you be okay?"

"I'll be fine. I'm going to damp mop the floor. Try to erase the image of those slithering snakes. Then maybe I'll be able to sleep." She turned to go inside wishing the lump in her chest weren't so large.

"Deni, wait." Joel rushed up the steps. "I know there isn't anyone in the house, but, I'd like to show you. We'll check the closets together."

The lump shrank. "Would you please?"

Holding tight to Joel's hand, Deni let herself be led room by room.

🐐

Deni opened her grandmother's rosewood jewelry box. The list she had made some time ago sat on top. She forgot about the necklace and unfolded the pale pink paper.

"The perfect man. I will not date and/or consider marrying anyone that:

1. Does not have faith in Jesus Christ as a personal Savior.

2. Does not like dogs, cats, and children.

3. Has been married before, unless there is a believable reason why his marriage didn't work.

4. Isn't supportive of my art.

5. Doesn't like cotton candy."

She added number five after Rob took her to a circus. She spotted the pink cotton candy, her favorite, right away. Rob refused to buy it for her. So she did. He wouldn't even eat a tiny piece of the fluffy stuff, claiming it to be too sticky, and a worthless treat. She had told him he was un-American and didn't know how to have fun.

Frowning, she shoved the list back into the box. Maybe she should add another caveat. Never date a man who wants your property.

CHAPTER SEVEN

The hot afternoon sun cast its rays on Deni's face. The heat couldn't evaporate the chills that ran down her spine. She stood a safe distance away from the house as Chad destroyed the overgrown rose bush that hid the foundation. Every time he pulled a thorny branch away, she jumped, expecting thousands of snakes to slither from underneath the ancient bush.

"Do you think you'll be able to find out where the snakes managed to get inside?" Her stomach rolled. She never wanted to see twitching snakes on her floor again.

"There could be a hole in the foundation. The problem with cinder blocks is that they erode sometimes." He stopped working on the rosebush, stood and rubbed his lower back. "Could be they've made a nest under the back porch."

"A nest." Deni shivered. How many babies did snakes have? Hundreds? "How will . . . Can you get them out of there?"

"Easiest way is to take off the porch. Be expensive to replace."

"But the alternative is worse. I can't have snakes crawling around in my kitchen."

Deni rubbed the back of her neck. "I suppose you should tear off the porch. If you want the job, that is."

"Sure, but it will take me longer to get to your studio." Chad shrugged. "Makes no difference to me."

"I can use the garage the way it is. Can you finish both the porch and the garage before it turns cold?"

"Maybe. Depends on if you want to replace the porch with wood again or order concrete formed steps, you can get those with a bigger landing. Think of it as a small porch. If you order them now they could be delivered in a day or two."

Calling the small patch of concrete, a 'porch' didn't seem to fit. It was more of a 'stoop' and served the purpose of a place to stand and unlock the door. "I think I want it to wrap around to the back. How would we do that?"

"Ask Joel. He's good at designs." Chad leaned over and pulled out the straggling rosebush roots.

"I will. At least I'll find out if I can afford to put on a real porch. As for the studio, I could buy a kerosene heater if you don't finish soon enough."

"Sure you want to put this kind of money into this house? What if you decide to leave? It would be a shame to tear down a new porch."

"I'm not moving." She should get a t-shirt with that printed on the front and back.

"Whatever. As long as you have money to pay me. Joel does want this place, though."

"How long have you two been friends?"

"Since kindergarten. We lost touch after high school. I married Mandy, and Joel went to college. He just moved back a few years ago."

"He told me your wife died. I'm sorry. Was it recently?"

"Yeah. Last year. She had breast cancer." Chad picked up a cluster of thorny stems. "I'll start a pile and haul them off later."

Deni waited for Chad to return from the side yard. She burned with questions to ask him about Joel. She felt a twinge of guilt; maybe she shouldn't ask Chad to talk about his best friend.

Chad walked with stooped shoulders, no joy on his face, only sadness. He stopped next to her, pulled a red bandanna from his back pocket and wiped the sweat from his forehead.

"How did Joel meet Ann? I don't remember her talking about him."

"One summer, Joel needed money, so he hired on with the newspaper as a paper boy. Ann liked him because he didn't throw the paper at the top of the hill.

He rode his bike down here and put it on her doorstep."

Ann would have appreciated the extra time it took Joel to do that.

"She always fed him something good to eat, like cookies or cake," Chad smiled. "Sometimes I did his route for him. Ann made the best soft and chewy oatmeal raisin cookies."

"So he's known her longer than me. I stayed with her one summer." Troubled, Deni thought about Ann and the many discussions and conversations while drinking chamomile tea. Had Ann had been afraid that Deni would fall back into a deep depression again. Or, did Ann indeed want Deni to start her business?

"I've tried to remember you but can't."

"I never left the house. My grandmother died, and at the time, it felt like I did too. Ann was my grandmother's friend. She was so good to me. She made me comfort foods like mashed potatoes and macaroni and cheese. She left me alone when I needed time by myself. After a few months, she decided enough was enough. She made me understand I was wasting the gift of life that God gave me, and it was time to use it."

"I know exactly what that's like. Depression." His voice was almost inaudible. "It's the blackest hole filled with murky water with something holding onto your ankles pulling you under. You just keep getting farther and farther from the light until all you can see is a tiny glimmer, like a far-off star." Chad paused. "Sometimes I think even that speck will soon disappear."

Tears filled Deni's eyes. "It doesn't have to be that way. Ann helped me through God's Word. Just knowing that He personally knew what it was like to lose someone made me feel better."

"Yeah, I've heard all that stuff before. Doesn't work for me. Seems God's good at taking away all of my hopes and dreams. I'm surprised He's let me have Doug this long." Chad bent down and brushed the dirt away from the foundation. "No holes here. The snakes must be under the porch."

Deni shivered, but did the goose bumps come from Chad's easy dismissal of God or the thought of slithering snakes?

Joel stared at the back of Deni's house. He walked from one corner to the other. He stopped to look toward the lake. She was right. A porch overlooking the lake would improve this place, but also make it more difficult for Deni to leave. Sitting out here watching the sunset would increase the value both monetary and emotionally.

Deni shifted her weight back and forth.

Joel smiled at her. "Have patience, I'm designing in my mind."

"Can you come up with something that won't cost a lot? I don't have much to spend right now."

"Guess it depends on how big you want to make it and what you have in mind." Joel watched her wind a curl around her finger. He remembered how soft her hair had felt on his chin and the way it smelled of lavender and mint.

"I'd love an old-fashioned screened-in porch. But I'd like to install windows so I can sit out here on fall and spring days." Deni smiled. "You'll need to include a place for a window that I made, too. I want the kind of porch with the white wicker rocking chair set at just the right spot to see through the trees to the lake."

"Sounds like you've thought about this quite a bit." Joel pointed toward the trees. "I don't think you'll be able to see the lake through all of those trees, even in the middle of winter. When I was little, there weren't as many. You could see the island from here."

Joel handed one end of the tape measure to Deni. "Take that end and hold it at the edge of the house." He watched her walk away. Odd that she always dressed in long pants or a skirt. Even today with the temperature in the nineties, she had on jeans and a T-shirt. She positioned the edge of the tape on the corner of the house, pressed with her thumb and held it flat with her fingertips.

"Okay, let it go." He pulled a pad of paper out of his pocket, removed a pencil from behind his ear, and wrote down the number. "Now, show me how far out you want the porch to go."

Deni walked about ten feet from the house. "I think this will be big enough. Were you planning on cutting down the trees when you built your resort?"

"Thinning them out is what I had in mind, with maybe a clear path or two where the lake would be visible."

"So the tree tops would overlap and frame the lake?" Deni made a canopy over her head with her hands.

"Exactly. Ann's driveway used to look like that until the power company cut them away from the lines. Her house was my last stop to deliver papers and the best stop on my route."

"Did you only have to work in the summer?"

"Nope, winter too. My dad drove me when the wind chill dropped below zero. The breeze off the lake in January can be brutally cold. Too cold to ride a bike."

"I can't wait for winter." Deni hugged herself. "I'm looking forward to bonfires on the shore, ice skating on the lake, wearing red woolen mittens and sipping hot chocolate."

Her face flushed as she talked. Her voice like joyful music. He imagined her twirling on ice skates, falling, her wild hair spilling out of her cap. He saw her sitting on the ice laughing. His throat tightened. He wanted to be in the scene with her.

"They have one or two skating parties on the public beach once the ice is thick enough." Joel managed to swallow the longing in his heart. He forced himself to look away from her and the image she'd created. "I need to measure the window that you want to use, also. Where is it?"

"It's in the studio."

"The studio?"

"In the garage. It's will be my studio when Chad finishes it. I've wanted one forever, so I decided I would start calling it the studio instead of the garage. I'm making a sign to go over the door. Glass from the Past. What do you think?"

"Not a bad name." Her face lit when she talked about her business. Did she know how pretty she looked? "Will it be made in stained glass?"

"Lots of blues, gold and reds. I have it drawn out, and some of the patterns are made. I hope to have it finished by next week. Come on, I'll show you."

Inside the studio, Joel blinked to adjust to the dim room. Behind him, Deni flipped on the overhead light. A gooseneck lamp perched on a long table at one end of the studio. Clear plastic safety glasses hung on a crooked nail pounded into the edge of the table.

He pictured her kneeling on the floor, with hair falling on her face. Would she chew her lip in concentration? Pound the nail until it cried for mercy, then bent over in agony like his sisters did?

"I know there's a lot of work to be done in here yet." Deni rested against a bare stud. "I want Chad to insulate and put up the dry wall before winter. Or at least I did before I found out I need a porch." She grimaced. "I hope a heater will keep me warm enough."

"Why don't you set up in one of the spare rooms? Then you wouldn't need to fix this place, and you would be warm."

"I did that in the apartment, but I was always afraid of the glass pieces. Those tiny slivers spread everywhere. They cling to my clothes and shoes, even though I'm careful. Not to mention Marmalade's curiosity. She's nothing but trouble when it comes to bottles and jars to swat."

Joel inspected the drawing Deni tacked to the wall. "Glass from The Past is going to be in red letters?"

"Outlined in gold and surrounded by blues. I'm going to use Cathedral Glass."

"You have glass from a church?"

"Cathedral Glass is a type of glass. It doesn't come from a church. Here, I'll show you." Deni handed him a fragment of semi-transparent blue glass. "This is cathedral glass and this," she gave him another piece, "is streaky cathedral because it has a combination of two colors. Sometimes it has more."

"Is this the one you're going to use in the sign?" Joel held out the semi-transparent piece.

"Yes. I'm using what I have in my scrap box, so I have to be flexible in my choices." She took the glass from him and laid them on the back of the worktable.

Deni pointed to a corner hidden by boxes. "The window is back behind those."

"I guess you want me to move them?" Joel picked up the first box. "Where do you want me to stack them?"

"Just shove them to the side. Some of them have glass inside. Most of my tools are still packed along with old pattern books. I'm waiting until I can build shelves out of concrete blocks and boards."

"I did that in college. Worked great for me, too." He shoved the last box to the side. The window waited wrapped protectively in an old blanket.

She pulled his hand away just before he undraped it and held on.

Startled, he glanced at her. Why did she stop him? He rubbed his thumb over the top of hers, feeling tiny ridges etched on her skin. "Why so many scratches?"

"From the tiny shards of glass. They don't hurt. I have to pull the pieces out with tweezers." Her voice sounded subdued. Or scared. He wasn't sure which. There was an almost imperceptible note of pleading in her face.

"What is it, Deni? What's wrong?"

She ran her tongue over her bottom lip. "Not many people have seen this window. It's special to me."

Understanding came to Joel. "You're afraid I'll laugh at your work."

"It's hard to show a piece of my art to someone new. I've put my soul into this one."

Joel turned her to face him. "Look at me." He stroked her cheek. "I promise I will never laugh at anything important to you." He tilted her chin and brushed his lips over hers.

He meant it to be a quick reassuring kiss. That thought flew from his mind as her warm lips quivered and responded to his. He pulled her into a deeper kiss.

93

He gathered her hair into one hand, released it, and stroked her back.

She froze. "Stop. Please." Her face flushed. She wrapped her arms around her waist. "The window is under there. Just take the measurements. I'll — I'll see you later." She brushed past leaving behind a cooling rush of lavender.

"Deni! Wait!" He sprinted after her. The kiss shocked him too. "Talk to me!" She ran into the house and slammed the door. He knocked on the door. "Deni!"

She didn't answer.

He stepped back. Frustration filled him. He hadn't meant the kiss to be like that, but he couldn't deny its impact. He wanted her to leave this house. She knew that. How hypocritical he must seem. Why had he done it? And, what was he going to do about it now?

Back in the studio, he walked to the dimly lit corner and slid the time-softened blanket from the window onto the floor. He picked up the window and carried it into the light. Its beauty stunned him. She'd pieced in delicate pastels instead of the dark jewel colors he associated with stained glass. At first glance, it was a design of flowers. Looking closer, he observed the smaller details woven into each flower. He didn't understand how everything connected. There were ballet slippers, three birds, and a Bible.

Now that one made sense. He wondered if the ballet slippers went with the Bible verse on Deni's key chain. But why did she include the three birds?

After measuring the window, he put it back and covered it with the blanket, adjusting it until both sides were equally protected. He smoothed the corners then let it rest against the wall.

He stood in the studio doorway thinking about the excellent craftsmanship used to make the window. The glass was cut and joined with solder that was free of bumps. The choice of colors and glass told him she was an artist, not just someone that stuck pieces of glass together and called it art.

He had been looking for someone to put in stained windows in a client's house. Now he found one. Living next door in the house that he wanted. It would be a tough decision. If he hired her, the lake property would no longer be in his future. Deni would have enough money to continue living next door, and the business she would attain from the display houses would only make Glass From the Past, grow.

The memory of Deni's warm lips and the hunger she responded with gave him another idea. Maybe there was another way to solve this problem.

Deni paced her bedroom floor, a diet soda in one hand and the phone in the other.

"But he kissed me, Lori. What was I supposed to do?"

"Kiss him back?"

Deni remembered the fire that soared from her lips to her toes. "I did. At least I think I did."

"You don't remember?"

"It was wonderful. It's kind of a blur. It happened so fast." She plopped on the bed. "He was about to pull the cover off the window-"

"You showed him the window?"

"Not exactly. He kissed me, and I had to get out of there. I left him there to look at it. I have to protect myself. Remember my list? And the fact that he wants me to leave?"

Lori's shriek came through loud enough for Deni to pull the phone away from her ear. "Trash that list!"

"I can't. This list will work. I know it will."

"Seems like he already meets the first qualification."

"I suppose, but then I thought Rob was a Christian, remember?" Back to pacing, she peeked out the window. "Joel's still in there, looking at the window. No, wait. Oh, no."

"What?"

"He's coming to the house. I'll talk to you later." Deni slid the phone in her back pocket and ran down the stairs.

The top of his head bobbed above the curtain on the door. How could she explain her reaction to his kiss? That she didn't want to get involved with him?

It seemed to Deni that Joel stood knocking at her door for an eternity. Her heart beat twice as fast as it should. Her mind raced with thoughts of the kiss. Her blood warmed. He did say he'd never laugh at her work. She wanted to trust him, but could she?

Should she?

🐐

"Joel?" Deni stood on the porch, the softness of dusk swirling around her, giving her an ethereal look. The way she spoke his name with a hint of softness and a question like she wanted reassurance. That he could give her, something he wanted to give her.

He wanted to run and grab her in his arms. Stroke her hair and kiss her until she realized he wasn't someone to be afraid of. Snap out it. Remember you're a Christian male so act like one. Maybe she should run the other direction.

"Are you okay? Why did you run off?" Joel started toward her.

"I guess. What about the window?" Deni's voice cracked.

"The window is spectacular. I can see why you want to include it in your porch. Some of the details I didn't understand. Will you explain them to me?"

"No." She shook her head, like a child. "I can't tell you what the window means to me, at least not yet. Maybe someday." Deni sat on the step. "Can we talk?"

"Sure." The narrow space offered Joel no other choice but to sit close to her. His arm brushed against hers. He wanted to pull her closer to him but somehow knew that would be wrong for her. "Are you going to tell me why you ran? Was it the kiss that scared you?"

Deni looked away. "I'm not sure. I was nervous about showing you the window, and I didn't expect the kiss."

Joel chuckled. "I didn't either." Or for the window to be that outstanding.

Deni faced him. Her eyes drew him into her soul. He was caught like an ant in the sugar bowl just as the lid closed over it. He wanted her, now—and for the rest of his life. He swallowed hard. "Are you trying to tell me I need kissing lessons?"

"No." The word came out so quiet he almost missed hearing it.

He smiled and tilted her chin. "You don't need lessons either." Giving her time to back away, he approached. He brushed his lips against hers.

Deni sighed. "Joel."

He didn't let her continue. He pressed his lips against hers harder. Heat rushed through him, and he was sure his body would sear itself into the concrete steps. Too much, too soon. Starting a relationship with her when he wanted her house was wrong. He pulled away and cleared his throat "It's probably best if I go now."

She nodded.

He gave her shoulder a soft caress. "I'll see you later."

CHAPTER EIGHT

Joel's day started later than usual. He'd have to work tonight on the house plans for the Fosters. They were good clients, and he wanted to do something different for them this time. He had already designed and built one house for them. Now they wanted another. In fact, the plans he was considering would have the perfect place for the installation of a few stained-glass windows. He knew they would like the idea. What kind of window could Deni design for them? Would she even be interested in something like this? The Fosters had unusual tastes, though, ranging from collecting antique jewelry boxes to an antique key collection.

As he drove past Taylor's Dance Academy, he noticed Deni's Jeep parked in front. Did she take dance lessons? Maybe that's why there were ballet slippers designed into the window. But why wouldn't she want to tell him that she danced? Why would that be personal? The Jeep had to be hers, he slowed as he drove past. Bright red with Missouri license plates. Definitely hers.

Why hadn't she put on her Illinois plates yet? Maybe she wasn't as sure about living here as she said. His heart lurched. What if she did leave? After last night he didn't want her to go anywhere. At least not until he knew where his feelings were headed. That's why he ran late this morning. He'd tossed and turned all night thinking about her and then wrestling with wanting her to move for his own selfish reasons. At one point he must have fallen asleep since he woke up sweating, thinking she had moved, and he couldn't find her. In the dream, he searched every stained-glass studio in the United States.

Pulling into his reserved parking spot on the side of Anderson Architects, Joel made a decision. He would follow his heart first. Deni was worth more to him than her property. His shoulders lightened. Maybe with her, he could find peace within himself and with God. Deni had an ease with God that he wanted for himself. A few times, he caught her talking to God as if He was her best friend. That's what he wanted, but he was afraid that he hadn't worked hard enough to have that kind of relationship with God.

Deni out of the hot sun into the cool studio waiting room thankful the dance instructor was willing to give her private lessons during the day. Dancing was as important to her as designing her windows.

A threadbare carpet held a round table, covered in magazines, in the center of the room. In the corner stood a display holding fancy leotards and chiffon skirts. In one corner a rattan basket full of used dance shoes threatened to explode.

"Hello? Anyone here?"

A smiling woman popped out from behind a door. "Hi, I'm Mary. Are you Deni? I was packing recital costumes in boxes. Those girls are never excited about putting them away. It's more fun to drag them out."

"My favorite was getting to dress up like a ladybug." Deni laughed. "It took my grandmother forever to sew on all those black dots."

"It seems like costumes were simpler in the past. Now they all want to be glitz and shine, except for the tiny little girls. They just want to have a 'ballerina skirt.' They want to look pretty when they spin."

"And then they see the older girls and change their minds, right?"

"Right. This year we had silver boots and alien antennas. The dressing room is down the hall. When you're in there, you'll see the door to the studio. I'll meet you there about five minutes."

Sitting on a white bench in the dressing room she slipped off her leather sandals and slid into her ballet slippers. She nudged the elastic band, snapping it in place on top of her foot. Standing, she pulled her denim jumper over her head, folded it, picked up her street shoes and stuffed everything inside her dance bag. Uncertain for a moment if it would be okay to leave it on the floor, she decided not to break an old habit and put the bag into one of the red cubbies that lined the wall.

At home, she'd put on the traditional ballet outfit of a black leotard and pink tights. She tied on a black skirt covered with tiny pink rosebuds.

Noticing a sign surrounded by posters of dancers, she read. "Warning! In this studio these items are illegal: earrings, necklaces, watches, rings, and bracelets. Remove before entering the dance studio or you will be sent off the floor. Hair must be controlled, not flying loose. Ask your dance instructor if you are in need of a rubber band."

The door to the studio creaked open. "Are you ready to dance?"

"Almost. I still need to tie my hair back. I wouldn't want to be sent off the floor."

"I wouldn't have sent you back. It's the teenage girls trying to be individuals that get my ire up. They have trouble understanding ballet classes are not the place to be different from everyone else."

"Funny, as a teenager I always wanted to be like everyone else. Maybe things have changed." She slipped her hair into a ponytail holder and then stuck her bag into a cubby.

The studio was quiet, not at all like in the evening hours when little girls gathered in huddles, making faces in the mirrors and giggling. Her leather slippers whooshed as she walked across the honey-gold wood floor. The room smelled of fresh paint. The white walls reflected in the mirrors at each end of the room. A few posters of dancers of varying ages decorated the walls.

Windows faced the street, but heavy drapes covered them. Was to keep people from looking in or to keep the cold and heat from entering through old windows?

Twisting the hem of her skirt in one hand, Deni asked, "Did Jena call you...about my leg?"

"Yes, she asked about my training and my students before she recommended the studio. She also told me a little bit about you. Don't worry. We'll go slow. No jumps or leaps so you won't re-injure yourself. How long have you been dancing?"

"Since I was three, but when I was sixteen, I stopped."

The twisted metal frame of Lane's car flashed into Deni's mind, fresh as if it had just happened. She pushed the memory back, deep where she wanted it to stay. "My grandmother convinced me to return to dance when I was twenty. I'm thankful that she did. Hard as it was and still is."

"I'm glad you didn't give up. It's good for the soul. Let's start with barre work." She led the way to the wooden bars mounted at the end of the room.

Deni followed, her skirt brushing against her thighs.

It was scary starting with a new teacher. What if she wanted more details about her accident than she wanted to give? Maybe Jena, her last teacher, explained all of it already.

"Fifth position, please."

Deni pushed her right heel to the left and snugged it into her left big toe. She wiggled her right foot to make sure she had the correct placement.

"We'll do three demi plies and one grande. Then we'll switch sides." Mary counted as she bent her knees, lowering her torso.

Deni followed Mary's count. Warm up came easy, unlike the center floor work that would follow. Would Mary be tough on technique? It would be hard to take criticism from an instructor that didn't know how far she had come, even if that is what she requested.

Mary moved Deni's shoulders back a tiny bit. "There, stand for a moment and feel this position. That is where the shoulders need to be. Lift your chin."

She struggled to maintain the correct posture.

"Jena told me what routine you were working on when you left her studio. I'd like to see what you remember and how you perform the steps. Kind of a test. But I promise not to grade you." Mary turned on the music and increased the volume.

Deni soon lost herself in the rhythm of the familiar music, moving across the floor feeling the moves, not just remembering them, until the last note ended.

"Good job. You've worked hard today." Mary smiled. "You are more advanced than you led me to believe. Next week we'll move on to more difficult movements."

Deni groaned. "If only dancing was as easy as it looks."

"Then everyone would be full of grace and dance to the music in their heads, and I would not have a job." Mary laughed. "Let's do as few cool down stretches on the floor before you leave."

Deni sat with spread legs and leaned to one side.

"What kind of work do you do that allows you to take off in the afternoon?"

"I'm self-employed." Deni switched sides. "Or will be when enough money starts coming in. Right now, I'm living on my savings account. Grand plans fill my dreams, though. I build and design stained glass windows. This morning I decided I needed to generate income. Now. So I'm going to advertise for students and hold classes at home."

"I know how it is to run a business. Lots of expenses. Even things like insurance, that I never thought of." Mary slid both hands along the floor through her spread legs. "Reach."

"I hadn't thought about that. I noticed an agent's office when I drove into town. Before going home, I'll stop by and ask him." Great. Another bill to pay before she even started making money.

"That should be enough of a cool down." Mary took off her ballet slippers and tossed them into a corner that held jazz and tap shoes. "You must have a large house if you're going to hold classes there."

"I'm in the process of turning my garage into a studio. I live down by the lake, about three miles from town."

"That might be too far from town. It would be difficult in the winter for students to get to you. There are a few empty store fronts on Third Street. Why don't you check into those and see what they would cost to rent?"

"That's true. I need to have classes this winter." The calculator clacked away in her brain. Renting in town would give her access to more students, but the cost? Could she afford it? She refused to give in to feelings of hopelessness. She would make this work, somehow, some way.

Deni closed the door to the insurance agency behind her. Maybe walking would help her mood. The quote was high because of the high risks using glass and soldering guns. Unless she used the Guilt Fund, and she wouldn't. She found herself standing in front of Anderson Architects. Maybe Joel would have the plans for her back porch. She wanted to see them but knew the work would have to wait. The studio had to come first.

She stepped back. He probably didn't have time to do them last night. She turned to leave, sad because Joel was the one person she wanted to share her disappointment about her financial obstacles. She wanted to hear his warm resonating voice tell her it would be okay, that people would line up to take classes from her. Then again, he might be happy to hear the news.

The door opened behind her, and she jumped.

"Excuse me! I wasn't paying . . . Deni?" Joel stood next to her. She sucked in the woodsy scent of his after-shave as she fought to regain her balance, but the delicious way he smelled made it difficult. "Were you looking for me?"

"No, not really. I was walking by and thought about lunch but—."

"But what? You decided you weren't hungry, or you didn't want to eat with me after all?"

"I didn't know if you would want to eat with me." She tripped over her words. "I mean, I didn't tell you I was coming to town, and you might have plans or already have eaten."

"I would enjoy having lunch with you. How about the Dixie Diner?" Joel's smile penetrated her body, warming her.

"Dixie Diner it is." Walking down the street, she was aware of his closeness. His presence made her feel safe. She wished he would hold her hand.

The diner resided in a brick two-story building. The gold plaque next to the door read Built in 1850. Joel opened the door for her. A sign stood in the entryway instructing customers to Please seat Yourself.

"Let's grab the corner table by the window. It should be quiet there." Joel touched the small of her back.

She crossed the red and white square floor tiles. Tablecloths of yellow stripes, blue flowers, and an occasional red bud covered the round tables. Each had a tiny white milk glass vase holding fresh flowers. Some tables had daisies, others carnations, and still others had red roses. Accordion folded napkins were stuffed into clear glasses.

"This doesn't look like a diner." She glanced up at the tin ceiling. "It's much too pretty."

He pulled out a white wrought-iron chair for her. "It didn't always look like this. The owners bought it a few years ago but kept the original name. They changed everything but the floor and the ceiling. The menu has everything from quiche to chicken noodle soup."

A young woman approached the table.

"Hi, Joel. You haven't been in for a while. I've missed your smiling face."

"Kathie, I'd like you to meet Deni. She's living out at the lake, next to me. She's opening a stained glass business."

"Nice to meet you, Deni. Good luck to you. Starting a business for yourself is harder than most people realize."

"Kathie, and her husband, Tim, bought the diner and remodeled it."

"This place is beautiful," Deni said.

"Thanks. Now, what would you two like for lunch?"

After Kathie left with their orders, Joel stared at Deni. She squirmed in her seat, knowing the time to talk about the other night had come. She grabbed her water glass and took a long drink. "I'm so thirsty from dancing."

"That was your jeep in front of Taylor's. I didn't know you're a dancer. That's why you have ballet shoes on the window, isn't it?" He looked pleased like he figured out an elusive puzzle piece.

"Yes, that's why." One of many reasons.

"Why you couldn't tell me that last night." Joel frowned. "Unless there is more to the story than dancing."

"There is, and I'd really like to tell you the rest of it, but I don't want to talk about it here. I'd rather enjoy lunch."

"Then tell me why you ran off when I kissed you the first time."

"I was confused." Deni's mind raced. Just how much should she share about Rob? What could she leave out? Her heart quickened. She blurted out, "I wasn't...I didn't expect you to kiss me."

"I didn't either. I'm glad it turned into a real kiss. But that still doesn't explain why you ran off. You could have slapped me, or told me never to do that again, but you ran. Why?"

"I'm sorry. You're right. It was too many emotions for me to process. You were about to see the window that only a few trusted friends have seen. Add that to the unexpected kiss and my feet took over. Kind of acted like a schoolgirl, didn't I?"

"Does that mean you don't want to...I'm really bad at this..." Joel reached across the table and touched the top of her hands. "What I'm trying to say is...is there someone else in your life? And if there isn't, would you like to see a movie or something?"

Heat crept up her face. He had no idea how much she'd like to take him home forever. "There was someone. His name was-is- Rob. We don't see each other anymore."

She searched Joel's eyes for courage and found a calmness she didn't expect. "Rob broke off our engagement. He said he didn't have a desire for me anymore. I don't want to feel wretched ever again. I'm not strong enough to survive anymore sadness of unfulfilled dreams."

"Why did — "

"Our dreams weren't the same."

Joel squeezed her hands. "I'm being selfish right now, but I'm glad he didn't marry you."

"What?"

"I'm glad because now we're both single. I'll try to understand if you say no, but please give me a chance?"

"I won't say no, Joel. For some reason, God put you into my life. I want to find out why." She warmed as he ran his finger at a snail's pace over her fingertips. "But I have to be sure it's me you want and not   the   property."

CHAPTER NINE

Deni sat in front of a wooden desk at the Sunshine Realty Company. The golden nameplate on the desk read Maureen Dunwoody-Top Seller 2014. How did Maureen make a living from this tiny space? There couldn't be many people buying homes, not in a town this size. Though the office was small and made her feel at ease. Every day brought new and interesting people and places to her attention, furthering her growing passion for this little town.

"Now, just let me take a look at what's available." Maureen pushed her glasses higher on her nose and peered at the monitor screen. "I think I have just the place for you." She turned her chair back to face Deni. "Want to take a look?"

Yes, so far, everyone she met welcomed her as if she was an old friend. Even the real estate agent. Except for Chad, of course. What would she do about him? Could she do anything to help him?

"Deni?"

"Oh, I'm sorry."

Maureen peered at the monitor screen as if addressing it, not Deni. "I think I have just the place for you."

"You do? Really? Is it close?"

Maureen turned her chair back around and squinted at Deni over her glass frames. "Shall we go over?"

Deni twirled a lock of her hair around her finger. "Shouldn't we discuss how much the rent is first? I won't be able to afford much."

"Let's not worry about that now. We'll play with the figures when we get back to the office." She brought out her black patent purse from under the desk and scooped up a set of keys.

Should she insist on knowing the cost before tromping off looking at something she might want but couldn't afford? Might as well look at it. "Can we walk there?" Deni tugged her purse strap onto her shoulder.

"We'll take my car. It will only take a second."

A moment later, Maureen pulled her luxury sedan in front of a sand-colored brick building. "This location would be perfect for you. With the dance studio down the street, you might pick up a few parents as students. It's always nice to be able to do something for yourself while you're waiting for a child."

Maureen unlocked the door. "I always read or wrote letters to friends while I Waited for my daughter to finish her lessons."

Deni eyed the huge plate-glass windows in front of the building as the real estate agent rambled. "Those are enormous display windows. I could put several pieces in each one."

"Wait until you see the inside."

The wooden floor was covered with a layer of dust, old newspapers, and a few empty soda cans.

Maureen kicked a few papers aside. "It's been empty for quite some time. The last renter had a bead shop. A bead shop, can you imagine? She had all sorts, some of them sold for over a dollar each."

"A lot of people make their own jewelry. I've made a few pieces myself."

"This is the main room. This way to the back." Maureen strode toward a small doorway.

Deni took another look around before following. There would be plenty of room to set up displays. She would need to paint. She ran her hand down the dull green wall. Dust fell, revealing a paler green beneath. Maybe she could just wash them, but the right shade of gray would set off the displays better.

The exposed wooden ceiling joists would be strong enough to hold windows for sale. She could aim track lighting to hit the glass imitating the sun, illuminating the clear and muted colors of the glass and casting rainbows on the wooden floor.

"Come along, now." Maureen called from the back of the store. "I think you'll find this spot interesting."

Maureen stood in a room lined with worktables and fluorescent lights.

Deni's heart beat faster. "A workshop! All I need are some stools. There's enough room here for..." She counted spaces in her mind. "At least ten students."

"I thought you would like this part." Maureen smiled. "There's more. Would you like to see?"

"More? How could there possibly be more?" Deni followed Maureen through another doorway. A partition divided the room, and one side held shelves for a storeroom. Glancing over the partition, Deni saw a small kitchen. An open door revealed a bathroom.

Deni twisted a lock of hair around her finger. "I really want to rent this place, but I don't know if I can afford it. I don't even have any students yet."

Maureen stood with her arms folded across her chest. "Well, you could rent it on a short lease, maybe six months."

"Six months? That would be enough time I'm supposed to get the studio going. But what if I don't get enough students? If I stay at the lake house with the studio, and I don't get any students, I'll still have the studio in six months."

"Your house isn't in a good location for a business, though, not if you want students. It's out of the way, and when the weather gets bad here, no one likes to drive to the lake. The wind is too strong, and sometimes the roads become impassable from the drifts. Have you checked with the high school? You could offer classes through their evening community class program."

Deni grinned. "Good idea! I hadn't thought of that. I'll check with them and see if it's a possibility. Then if I can afford to rent this building, I'll get back with you."

At home, Joel held a bottle of pain reliever in his hand. He pushed and then twisted off the childproof cap, plopped two of the extra strength pills into his mouth and swallowed them without water.

Having lunch with Deni gave him a headache. She was a ball of confusion, tangled and knotted. He was determined to find out everything about her. He knew he was falling in love with this brown-haired spitfire. He needed to find a way to prove to her that she was what counted in his life. But he had convinced her that he wanted her to leave the cottage. That much was still true. Now he would have to prove that he wanted her to stay. But how?

Opening the freezer door, he played the game of what's for dinner. Frozen burritos didn't appeal to him and neither did chicken fried rice. Pizza would do. Trashing the box and plastic that covered the cold food, he slid the pizza into the oven. He set the timer and hoped by the time it went off his aching head would feel better.

His mind in a fog, he entered his home office and sank back into the desk chair. He sat swinging the seat from side to side, then rolling it back and forth.

He could give up building the resort. His gaze landed on the Victorian model, and the chair came to a stop. She'd never believe that.

Could he sacrifice a lifetime dream for a woman?

A woman full of secrets.

Why didn't she want to talk about her dancing?

And what did those three birds in the window mean?

The oven timer chimed as someone knocked on the screen door.

"Just a sec. I'm coming."

Chad strode though the door. "It's me."

"You're in time to share a pizza, fresh from the oven." Joel waved Chad into the kitchen. "Grab a couple of plates, will you?"

"Sure. I had a free evening. Doug's at a friend's house. I called to see if you wanted to go into St. Louis and do something." Chad frowned at Joel. "You didn't call back."

"So you took a chance I'd be here?"

"Figured you were home. You don't do anything during the week unless it's with me." Chad slid the plates like hockey pucks across the kitchen table.

Joel hesitated, confused for a moment by the odd feeling of guilt. Or was it annoyance? "That's true."

"Why not?"

"I usually wait until after dinner to return calls." He had started that tradition after one client insisted on calling him at home every night for months.

"Great dinner." Chad shoved a slice of pepperoni pizza into his mouth. "Eat like this every day?"

"I'm sure you do better, right? Besides, I had a good lunch." He stopped, the guilt slammed into him again.

"With who?" Chad picked up a slice.

Joel waited until Chad finished, not wanting to risk his best friend choking. "I had lunch with Deni." "My plans have changed. I think about her all the time. I asked her to go out with me. I don't want her to move before I find out if she's the one I want to spend my life with." Joel forced himself to calm down. He didn't understand why Chad hated the thought of Deni staying.

Chad threw his pizza on the plate and stood. "If you won't get rid of her, I will. No matter what it takes."

Tired from dance class and the rush of excitement from finding the perfect building that she couldn't possibly afford, Deni collapsed onto the couch.

She should eat something with protein. Not that she was hungry. Lunch had been filling. Was it the lunch, the company, or the possibilities of her own workshop that dulled her hunger?

A feeling she was going to make this work sailed through her veins. She closed her eyes and whispered a quick prayer. "Thank you, Father. I know I have to trust You, and it will work out."

Feeling positive Deni leaped off the couch, scaring Marmalade. The cat streaked across the slick floor, howling. Hershey barked as he chased the cat and slid around the corner.

"Hershey, Marmalade's not playing!" The dog continued to chase after the cat. Laughing, Deni headed to the kitchen. After she fed her pets, she would grab a cheese stick and walk the beach to Joel's. Maybe he knew something about the building she'd found in town.

The sun dipped below the horizon as she closed the front door behind her. She loved this time of day. The golden light blurred all the sharp lines and details, giving the world the appearance of a watercolor painting.

As she walked the beach to Joel's, Deni tried to push her feelings back into place. He's just a friend-okay, a boyfriend. But I'm not going to be serious about him or anyone. There's no need to fall in love; I have everything I could possibly need in my life. I have more than I possibly need.

A quick measure of sadness hit her, maybe a nudge from God. I guess I don't have everything I want or need. I want to have a family. Does Joel? Would only wanted biological children like Rob? That was one of her greatest sorrows, the fact that something was taken from her that night of the crash.

She would never be able to have children, not with her body anyway. After all, she'd grown up without her mother and father and she came out just fine. She could love an adopted child as much as one she physically bore. Her grandmother had shown her how.

Still, she missed having her father. All those times when her friends talked about how their overprotective fathers didn't like the boys they dated. Maybe if her father had lived, she would never have been in the accident. Yes, she would like to have children, but she would like for them to have a father as well.

As she got closer to Joel's house, she spotted Chad's truck parked by the back door. Disappointed, she thought about turning back. She didn't want to share her news with Chad.

Loud, angry voices caught her attention. Making up her mind not to eavesdrop or go to the house, she turned to go.

"Deni? You can't be serious."

She stopped short. Serious about what? She stood still, trying to hear Joel's reply, but it was muffled.

"You want her to do windows? You know what that means! It's the end of our project." Chad sounded like a bull after a rodeo clown.

Deni shivered and decided to return home. She didn't want to know what they were arguing about, even if it did have something to do with her. She paused. What windows was Chad talking about? Was Joel thinking of asking her to design windows for him

Her heart lightened as she continued her walk home, though Chad's deep unhappiness refused to leave her mind. She promised herself she would pray for Chad to open his heart to God again.

🐐

Needing to get the argument with Chad off his mind, Joel laced on his running shoes and took off down the gravel road. Sweat poured from his brow and soaked his shirt. He didn't know if he felt better, but he was tired.

The full moon lit the night. He'd walk past Deni's and come back along the beach. After the other night, he wanted to reassure himself she was safe in her house.

The lights were on, but he didn't see anyone. Hershey barked once. Deni probably told him to be quiet. She was too trusting. She should at least look out the window and see if there was a reason for the dog to bark.

Approaching the water, he heard splashing. He stopped to listen. Someone was swimming. Deni? Swimming in the moonlight? He had never seen her get in the water. The first night she walked the beach edge with her pants rolled up but that was all. He had thought she might be afraid of the water.

Curious, he made his way onto the beach. Silhouetted by the moon, Deni rose out of the water but didn't see him. Joel's mouth went dry at the sight of her perfectly formed arms and waist. Her hair slicked back behind her ears, still curled on her back. Her one-piece suit revealed a muscled back.

His gaze traveled to her legs, legs he had never seen. The right one looked a little different from the left, but why? He squinted trying to figure it out. Her right leg was shaped-

Just then she picked up a beach towel and wrapped it around her waist. Joel blinked his eyes. It must have been the way the moonlight hit to cause that effect.

Joel went back up the path a little way to give her some privacy. He didn't want her to know he'd seen her getting out of the water. Or scare her. She wouldn't be expecting anyone on this part of the beach. He stomped his feet a few times, like he was running, and then ran onto the beach. "Hi," he gasped.

"Joel? You scared me." Deni straightened the dress she slid over her wet suit. "Do you always run at night?"

"Sometimes, if I have something on my mind." He picked up a smooth stone.

"Does that help you solve the problem?"

"Not always." Joel tossed the rock into the water. "Sometimes I get tired before I come up with a reasonable solution." He squatted on the shore edge, reached into the water, and splashed his face. "Water feels nice."

"It wasn't too cold tonight."

"Do you always swim at night?" Joel sat on the beach. "I don't think I've seen you in the water since you moved in."

"I try to swim every night when the moon is out. Tonight's was so bright that I didn't even bring a flashlight. Being around water relaxes me when I'm worried or anxious."

Joel patted the sand. "Want to sit for a little while and listen to the waves?"

She smiled, and his heart flipped.

Deni sat close enough to smell her hair. The desire to touch her overwhelmed him. He sought her hand in the moonlight and held it in his.

"Is Hershey being punished?"

Deni laughed. "No, I wanted a calm swim, not a rambunctious free-for-all in the lake with a water-loving Labrador."

"Poor Hershey, he has to stay all alone in the house while his mistress enjoys the water. Isn't that like sneaking out to do something by yourself when you know your best friend would like to go?" Joel pushed Chad's face from his mind. He had enough guilt for one evening.

"I gave him a bone. I'm sure he doesn't even miss me."

"How do you feel about sailboats? Would you like to go out onto the lake Sunday evening and watch the sunset?"

"You have a sailboat?"

"A client offered his to me." Joel had a fleeting thought of Chad racing down the driveway. Then dismissed it. "We can take Hershey along if you like."

"I'll go sailing with you if you go to church with me in the morning."

"Deal. Just tell me what time and where."

"I like going to the eight o'clock service in town. I'll pick you up at seven- thirty, okay?"

"Fine with me." He squeezed her hand. "What you did do with the rest of your day? Did you find a place to rent?"

"Yes, I did. I fell in love with this place just down from the dance studio. It used to be a bead shop."

"I know that building. At one time it was a farm shop. It has exposed rafters. The beams look like they may be made from cedar. Are you going to rent it?" Joel tried to keep the excitement out of his voice.

"I thought I would, but when I checked the mail, I found out I have to pay two thousand dollars in real estate taxes for this house." Deni's voice quivered. "I just don't know where I'll get the money to pay them. I would like to have the studio downtown. It makes better business sense if I want to have students."

"You have a few months to make the second payment." This new development would make Chad happy but made him hurt for Deni. "Maybe you'll get enough jobs before then."

"I don't know. I'm trying to trust God on this, but it's so hard sometimes. I think He wants me here, but so many problems keep coming up that I begin to wonder if I made the wrong choice." She moved away from Joel's. "I'm getting cold. Want to walk the beach with me?"

He stood and brushed his hair back. "Sure. How did you make the decision that God wants you to be here? Or is that too personal?"

"My life had been a mess for a while, and I've been asking God to fix it, send me somewhere away from where I was. Never ask God for something if you're not sure you want it."

"I don't get it. You think if you ask Him for something God will give it to you?"

"Not all the time, but sometimes He surprises you, and you end up doing things you never thought you would. Like opening a business." Deni giggled.

"Isn't that what you wanted?" Joel stooped down, picked up a rock and tried to skip it in the path of the moonlight. It sank.

"I thought I did, but I didn't know how hard it was going to be. That I would have to have insurance and maybe even a different studio. It sounded easy in the beginning. Just turn the garage into a studio and hang a sign." Deni sighed. "It's overwhelming."

He turned her to him. He tilted her face in the moonlight. Yes, tears clouded her eyes, just on the edge of spilling. "I know you can do this. You have a faith in God that I desire. He won't let you fall."

He wrapped his arms around her. Her damp head fit perfectly under his chin. She pressed into his chest, almost as if she couldn't get close enough. His throat tightened in his want for her. He would do anything for this woman. He wanted to protect her from anything that could cause her worry or harm.

He decided he would ask his clients, the Fosters about using stained glass. He wouldn't tell her until he knew for sure, though. She didn't need another disappointment.

"I'll hold you forever if that's what you want," he whispered into her ear.

CHAPTER TEN

The older pastor crept up to the pulpit. Joel's face burned when the pastor's eyes rested on him for a moment. There was no doubt, Pastor Benz remembered their last conversation about why he wouldn't be returning to church. He squirmed, thinking about how righteous he had been. Joel shook off the guilt. He was here now, though. That counted. Right?

Deni's hand brushed against his. Would she mind if—? Feeling a surge of bravado, he slid his hand over hers. His courage faltered as she pulled away, but then her fingers entwined with his. Elation filled him, and he found himself drawn into the pastor's words.

"That's right, folks. It's a free ride to heaven for all of you. Once you believe that Jesus died for your sins, that's it. You're on your way."

Joel sat straighter in the pew. This was something he hadn't heard before. There had to be more. Where did the work come in?

"Does that mean you don't have to do anything once you become a Christian?" Was Pastor Benz looking right at him.

Here it comes. He knew he hadn't misunderstood. Joel prepared himself for hearing how many things he still had to do before he would be accepted into heaven.

"You don't have to do anything. Not one thing."

What? Do nothing? He peered sideways at Deni. She didn't look surprised to hear this message.

"Helping someone will not gain you entrance into heaven. Only believing in Our Savior will do that. But..." The pastor looked around the church. "You will want to do work for God. You will be so filled with God's love and the Holy Spirit you will want to help people, to do those good works. But it is the love and grace of God that saves you. Nothing you do will change that."

Stunned, Joel glanced at the others in the church to see if they were shocked. Most of them seemed bored as if this was such an old message and they didn't need to hear it again.

Joel's knee bounced shaking the pew. How had he missed this?

Deni elbowed him and glared at his knee.

He stilled, hoping the service would soon end.

After the service, Deni and Joel stood in the fellowship hall. Joel checked his watch again for the fourth time in five minutes. He must not be comfortable. Despite the list, she had been hoping, even dreaming, that he could be the man on her list. He wasn't, and she would have to squash any feelings she had about him. Her heart grew heavy.

"We can leave in a minute. I need to talk to Mark Prentice. He's on the properties committee. He left a message on my answering machine to speak to him this morning."

"I'm fine. We don't have to rush out of here." He twisted his arm to look at his watch. "I need to talk to you about something."

"What about?" She looked closer and fought the urge to brush the side of his face with her hand. He seemed upset, but why? "We can leave now. I can call Mark later."

"No. I can talk to you later. Might even be better to wait when we're sailing."

A small group of teenagers pushed through the narthex, pushing Deni into Joel. He brought her close to him, holding her for just a second.

The musky smell of his after-shave filtered through her like a smoldering fire. What was wrong with her? This infatuation had to stop. He didn't even come close to making her list. Besides, he might even be the one who put the snakes in her house. Stop that, she told herself. He wouldn't have done that, no matter how desperate he was to have the property.

"Sorry." She stepped back, fanning her face with the bulletin. "Teenagers take a lot of room."

"Deni! I'm glad you haven't left yet." A dark-haired man stuck his hand out in front of Joel. "I'm Mark Prentice."

"Joel Anderson. I'm a friend of Deni's."

"Glad you came this morning." Mark turned to Deni. "I wanted to ask if you would make a window for our new nursery. The counsel thought something along the lines of Noah's Ark would be appropriate."

"Animals would be fun to work with in glass. Lots of colors and shapes." Deni twirled her hair between her fingers. "When would you need it?"

"We'd like it before the first of November. If you can squeeze us in. I know it's short notice. That's when we're planning to hold the dedication service." Mark turned to Joel. "Have you seen her work? She has a marvelous talent."

"She's amazing. The way she puts those intricate pieces together make her work ingenious."

"It's my gift from God that makes it possible any of the work." She warmed at Joel's compliment. "Mark, I can have the window done in time if I order the glass right away — that means we have to select the colors, and I have to get a design ready."

"Deni, the church wants to pay you for the work. We aren't asking for this as a gift."

"But — "

"No, we won't accept it as a gift. We know you're starting out and it's a tough beginning. We want you to succeed so you'll stay in our community and be a part of our church family."

"Thank you." Joy bubbled up inside her, her first sale, and to the church. "Maybe someday I can make another window as a gift. I'll call you tomorrow and set up a time to discuss this further."

"Fine," Mark said. "I see Mrs. Shelton. I need to speak with her, too. Joel, it's been nice meeting you. Hope to see you again."

Deni turned to Joel. Standing tall and dressed in a smoke gray suit, blue shirt and navy tie, he took away her breath. Concerned she had done or said something wrong to upset him she grabbed his hand.

"Come on." She pulled on his hand. She couldn't wait to find out what was bothering him. She tried to ignore the fiery sensation that roared through her. Funny, but when he held her hand in church, she felt safe and secure.

She led Joel to the side chapel. It would be empty. There they could talk undisturbed. Holding his hand snug in hers, Deni pushed open the heavy oak door to the side chapel.

"Not here." His face paled.

"Joel, what's wrong?"

The last time he'd been in here had been for Mandy's funeral. He didn't want to be here now, not even with Deni. He could still smell the flowers and see the panic and fear etched on Chad's face. The chapel was dark and a little chilly then. Today, a small ray of sunlight peaked through the window. A cloud chased the sun away, casting gray shadows over the altar as if God knew what he felt.

The stone walls closed in on him like a crypt full of death and despair. He tugged on Deni's hand, finding comfort in the way she held it so tight. "I can't be in here, not yet."

"I'm sorry. I thought it would be quiet here, and you could tell me what's on your mind." Deni reached out and touched his shoulder.

"Doesn't appear to me that way right now. It just isn't the place I want to be this morning." Joel jutted his chin out further. "I want to wait until we're on the lake."

Deni let go of Joel's hand.

"Deni, I know this doesn't make sense to you right now, but I don't want to be in here. I promise to explain it later. Please, don't be angry."

"I'm not." Deni shrugged.

"Good, then let's go." Joel led her back into the narthex.

"Joel Anderson? Is that you?"

Turning, toward the woman making her way toward them. He groaned inside. Just what he needed.

"Yes, it's me, Mrs. Tindall."

"It's so good to see you here again. Your mother will be thrilled to know you're coming back to church." She smiled at Deni. "Is she the reason for your return?"

"Mrs. Tindall, it's been nice seeing you, but we have to hurry right now. Perhaps we can talk more next time." Joel grabbed Deni by the hand and pulled her through the door.

On the ride home in the car, Deni was silent. Was she angry? Maybe? She clinched her hands in a death grip.

"Something wrong?"

"No, nothing."

"Are you sure?"

"Yes."

"Why aren't you talking to me?"

"I don't know what to say. Everything set you off this morning. And why did you pull me away from Mrs. Tindall? Are you embarrassed having a friend of your family meet me?"

"Whew, sure glad you aren't mad at me. You, glorious woman, do not embarrass me. Mrs. Tindall, on the other hand, might have by telling stories of my youth."

Deni's laughter relaxed him.

"I would have loved to hear about the younger you. I'm lucky there isn't anyone," Deni's voice broke, "to tell tales about me."

"Maybe I'll make up embarrassing stories and tell them to our friends." Joel reached over and rubbed under her chin. "Or I could just acquire new ones as I get to know you. I bet I could call your friend Lori and find out what she knows."

"Stop! Unfair!"

"Say 'uncle' and I'll quit."

"Uncle! You're a terror." Deni giggled and tugged on his shirtsleeve.

"So, you are going to let me wait until we get out on the lake?" Joel was happy to see Deni smiling again, not dwelling on her past.

"Well, maybe I'll let you wait that long, but I might have to start asking you as soon as we leave from the dock."

"Watch it. Your lack of delayed gratification is showing." He watched her arch her eyebrow and give him a look that would melt a third grader into their seat. "Sorry, teach!"

"You'd better be unless you want to sit in time out." She turned her face away from him, but in the reflection of the glass, he saw her grin.

CHAPTER ELEVEN

Deni stretched out in the sailboat, letting her hair hang over the edge. The late afternoon sun caressed her cheek with its warm kiss. The sun warmed her legs through her white linen slacks. Not for the first time she wished she could wear shorts.

"Deni?" Joel's buttery voice slipped into her thoughts.

"Umm?" She sat and dangled her hand over the edge of the boat watching the emerald water float through her fingers.

"I thought maybe you were asleep. I didn't want you to burn." He adjusted the jib.

"No, not asleep, just enjoying the sunshine on my face. Deni lifted her hand and watched the rainbow filled beads of water drip from her fingers. "Are you going to tell me what bothered you this morning?"

A small frown drifted over his face for an instant, then he smiled at her. "You didn't ask as soon as I thought you would, but then again, you did ask before we reached the island. I knew you wouldn't make it that far."

"Could you be stalling?" Deni put on her best teacher face. "It will be better for you to tell me instead of making me dig up the reasons myself."

"That is one scary face. Did it work on your students?" Joel opened the cooler. "Soda?"

"Water please, and then the story."

He brushed clinging ice from the bottle, twisted off the cap, and handed it to her.

"Thank you." She pressed the cold bottle to her cheek. "That feels good. Well, I'm waiting."

Joel laughed. "You win. I'll talk. You'll make a great mother. Nothing would get by you."

She blinked to keep the unexpected tears from rolling down her cheeks. She wanted so much to be a mother someday, but who would want to be married to someone as broken as she? Her heart twisted, and she pasted on a smile. "I would like that someday."

"I heard something this morning in church that I missed before. The pastor said we don't have to do anything to get into heaven. All this time, I thought we had to do something."

"Grace." Deni closed her eyes for a moment.

"I thought..." Joel touched her knee.

"You thought you had to work hard doing good things all the time?" She tried to ignore the warmth creeping from his hand. Stop it. This was serious stuff. How could she be thinking about her feelings when he needed to talk?

"I'm still not sure how it works. Can you explain it?" Joel rubbed his chin.

"It's simple, and yet it's the hardest thing for some people to understand. The only way to heaven is to believe Jesus died for our sins. That's it. Wait. That didn't sound like I wanted it to."

"I know I've heard about good works, though. The pastor even mentioned them in the sermon this morning."

"Works are real. They just don't get you to heaven all by themselves." Deni searched for the right examples in her life. "Maybe this will help you understand. In my heart and mind, I know God loves me. Not just loves me but loves me and accepts me like a lover."

"What?" Joel whipped around and stared at her.

"The book, Song of Solomon, tells me how God feels about me. It fills me with happiness and joy." Deni ran her finger around the top of her water bottle. "Do you remember the first time you fell in love?"

"Second grade. Janna Lyn. She always wore purple socks."

"Umm, I meant a little later in your life, someone you thought you couldn't live your life without?"

"In my junior year of high school, I fell in love with Kristin."

"Do you remember how you would do anything she wanted? I even mowed grass for a guy. I couldn't do enough for him."

"I get it. That's where the works come in. Loving God back makes you want to do things to please Him, right?"

"Yes. God's love moves you to love others. And then you begin to act out your love.

"But, I don't know if I can accept that. It seems too easy." He shook his head, "No, I'm not sure."

"Why couldn't you tell me about this in the chapel?"

"The last time I was there, I had to say goodbye to Mandy." He looked away.

"I'm sorry. I didn't know." Her heart clenched in sorrow. She wanted to reach out and pull him to her. Why God? Why did it have to be so hard for some?

The sailboat bumped against the homemade dock. A gentle wind rifled through the prairie grass on the beach. Rope in hand, he jumped onto the dock. He secured the rope around a post with chipped red paint.

"May I present the Island of Enchantment?" He bowed, extending his hand to Deni.

"An enchanted island! How beautiful." Deni stood and reached for Joel's. "Is there a local myth that goes with this place?"

"No. We could make one up, though. The truth is it isn't called the Island of Enchantment either. Chad and I played here in the summers. Its real name is Patamaw Island, but we changed its name many times."

"I can imagine what games you played here. Let's see. War games. Space game."

"Sometimes, and sometimes we played Indiana Jones. We made a snake pit once Chad collected sticks to toss in the bottom for pretend snakes."

She shuddered remembering the slithering snakes on her kitchen floor. "That's a game I could live without. Not my favorite movie either."

He climbed back into the sailboat for the cooler and the basket of food. He slid them onto the dock and then hopped up next to her.

"We have a little time to explore the island before we eat. I want to be back on the water and close to home to watch the sunset. Come on, let's see if the tree house is still there."

Deni followed Joel over the rocky beach. "How long has it been since you were here?"

"I came over about four years ago. I circled the island in the boat but didn't dock. Must be about six or seven years since I actually walked here." He turned down an almost invisible path.

A thorny bush snagged her pant leg. She bent down to pull it free only to catch the other leg in a bush behind her. She yanked it. The material ripped. She grimaced. Inspected the tear and sighed with relief to see it was small.

"Problems?" Joel stood a few feet away, clear of the thorny plants.

"Just a snag." She stood, gathered her hair in one hand and held it high, letting the breeze from the lake cool her neck. "Is it much farther?"

"It should be just ahead."

"I hope so. Isn't it about time to go back to the boat?" Her leg shot bolts of lightning from her calf to her thigh.

"Are you trying to tell me you aren't a wilderness woman?"

"I don't mind doing things outdoors. Just don't expect me to be Jane to your Tarzan." Her faced heated from the connotations that jumped into her mind. "I mean, uh, I don't like to be where there are hidden dangers, like snakes."

"Guess that means you aren't in love with me since you aren't willing to follow me into my jungle." He pretended to pout. "My charms must not have captured your heart."

"Could we go back, please? I'm hot, and I think you've had too much sun." She turned away so he wouldn't see the tears in her eyes.

Joel noticed Deni's limp as she walked to her house. Would she be angry if he asked if she were okay?

At the door, she turned to him. "I had a great time today. I like sailing, but I'm not so fond of hiking. An old injury--"

"What happened?"

She touched his lips with her finger. "I don't talk about it. I hope you don't mind. Some memories are better forgotten."

He wouldn't push her, not with that grief-stricken look on her face. His heart broke for her. He pulled her close. "You're beautiful. Meant to be kissed in the moonlight." His lips met hers. The kiss deepened. He lingered, hating to break it off.

Then Hershey barked, and the moment dissolved.

CHATPER TWELVE

Deni glanced at the time on her phone. She'd been on hold for less than five minutes, but it seemed much longer. The glass for Noah's Ark should have been here a week ago and not being able to work on it would put her in jeopardy of not finishing the window in time for the nursery dedication. She envisioned a lot of long days and late nights to get it done.

"Ms. Sparks, thank you for holding." The man with a thick India accent continued. "I have the receipt. The glass was delivered on the tenth of this month."

"I didn't get the shipment on any date." Her grip on the phone tightened.

"I have a copy of the signed receipt."

"That's impossible." Her heartbeat quickened. "Who's name is on it?"

"A Dennis Spark accepted the package."

"There isn't a Dennis Spark!" She paused, taking a deep breath to calm down. "Could you email me a copy? I don't understand who signed it. I'm the only one here."

"Yes, I can do that."

"What do you do in cases like this? Do you re-send the order?"

"Yes, I can do that for you. Will you be using the same account to purchase this order?"

"Isn't it covered by insurance?" This couldn't be happening. Her bank balance had dribbled to almost nothing.

"Insurance covers breakage and packages delivered to the wrong place. In this case, the glass was accepted at the correct address. So, no ma'am it is not eligible for a free replacement."

"It wasn't accepted by me. I'm Denise Sparks, not Dennis Spark. Who could have signed?" She walked faster across the floor.

"That I can't tell you. But there isn't anything we can do on this end. Would you like to re-order? We can express ship it to you, or overnight it for an extra charge."

"No. Not right now." After hanging up, Deni sank to the kitchen floor. Marmalade crawled into her lap and she stroked the cat. Who had signed for her package? Joel? No. He would have told her besides he hadn't been here for several days. She would have suspected him if things hadn't been so perfect. Or was it perfect because he knew she wouldn't have the supplies she needed?

The screen door allowed a gentle warm breeze to flow into the kitchen. The edges of discarded envelopes and bills gently riffled with the wind, casting the scent of an advertised perfume card through the room.

Deni sat with her elbows propped on the table edge, her chin resting in her hands. She watched the paper move. If only the bills would disappear in the breeze.

Using a steno book, she once again wrote down her expenses and the money she had from her last paycheck. She didn't want to, but she might have to cash in her small retirement fund. It couldn't be worth much, as she hadn't taught long enough to build it to a large sum. It would take time to withdraw the money, too. Maybe a month or more. Or she could use the Guilt Fund. No, using it meant she was okay with her parents dying in that plane crash. And she wasn't. Frustrated, she stood and threw the pen on the table.

The glass-fronted cabinet with its showcase of snack foods beckoned. Something crunchy would be good. Maybe that would release the tenseness from her aching jaw. Stuffed in the back of the pantry, behind an opened box of cereal, she found a bag of hard sourdough pretzels. They would do. She tossed the bag on the table then looked in the almost barren fridge for a diet cola.

Pretzel between her teeth, she paced the floor, wondering what to give up, what she could give up.

Her bag sitting by the back door caught her eye. Dance lessons. She could give up those. Or could she? Now would be a good time to quit since she'd only gone the new studio a few times.

Her grandmother urged her to go back to dancing. She rubbed her leg. No, she couldn't give up the lessons, not when they made her feel better.

Selling the Jeep would help, but if the weather forecasters were right, the winter was going to be a bad one. "A winter to rival 1982." The paper ran interviews with people from that famous winter who had been stranded for days. The National Guard had been called out to bring pregnant women to the hospitals and to pick up doctors. The interstates were closed. Without the Jeep, she'd never be able to get up the drive to the road. Not in a winter like that.

Cutting back on food wasn't an option. As it was, she hardly spent any money at the grocery store. Her one weakness there was her fondness for ice cream sandwiches. Books were another. She could give up the ice cream. Better for her hips anyway. But without books, what would she do with her evenings? Her mind drifted to the last few nights and the time she spent with Joel. If last night was any indication, she might be able to give up books forever.

Closing her eyes, she could feel the warmth of Joel's lips. The evening ended with that powerful kiss. He looked as surprised as she had felt when he backed away from her. He stood, put his hands in his pockets, and said maybe they should talk later. Still reeling from his kiss, she didn't say anything. She just stood there watching his taillights disappear into the darkness.

This morning she realized she no longer had a choice. She would have to tell Joel about Rob. But one thing was for sure. She was not going to tell him exactly why Rob broke off their engagement.

Her conscience jabbed her in the middle of her back. Wouldn't that be lying to keep the truth from Joel? She shrugged the off the sharp finger of guilt. She'd tell him, later. That is, if they became seriously involved. No sense dragging the past out and reliving it if there wasn't a need.

With a heavy sigh, she returned to the task at hand. "Okay, no ice cream sandwiches and no new books. I'll use the library."

Tapping on the cold soda can, she tried to come up with another way to cut expenses. "What I need is a way to bring in some extra money until I sell a few more windows."

Grabbing the pad of paper and pen off the table, she began another list: substitute teach, work at the fast food place, deliver newspapers. None of those looked appealing. She didn't like the uncertainty of teaching in a new classroom every day. She wasn't good at waiting on people, and she didn't like getting up early in the mornings. She scratched them out until the black ink obliterated the words.

What she really wanted to do was play in her studio arranging bits of colors like a patchwork quilt. Her creative mind had been pushing her to get busy, at least make a few small items. She couldn't afford the building in town, but she could offer classes this summer.

She scribbled down projects that her clients could make. Sun catchers and small desk displays would be easy for beginners. It wouldn't cost much for supplies since she had boxes of small pieces of glass left from previous projects. With renewed enthusiasm and excitement, she hadn't truly felt since coming to live at the lake, Deni sprang from the chair, the list clutched in her hand. She had work to do.

🐕

The halogen lamp illuminated Deni's workshop. The bright light chased the darkness from the garage corners and from Deni's mind. She reached into a ceramic vase for a pencil, ready to work before thoughts of Joel crept back into her heart.

Pencil in hand she sat, head bent, sketching on the pattern card she would use to cut the pieces of glass for the ark. At least those would be done.

A mulberry-scented candle flickered as a small CD player mourned an old blues song. Deni dropped the pencil on her desk, closed her eyes and allowed her body to sway with the sound. She wished she could have Joel's arms around her. She'd like to lay her head against his chest and feel the rhythm of his body. Stretching her arms in a circle, she imagined his beating heart under her cheek. Would she ever allow herself to discover what it was like to dance with him? She sighed as the last notes of the song died away. She forced her thoughts back to the job at hand.

She glanced at the window-sized drawing of Noah's Ark hung above her worktable. She finished it last week, liking it enough to buy a box of forty-eight crayons and a pack of new markers. With child-like glee, she spent several evenings coloring the zebras, peacocks and even added butterflies to the scene. Filling in the peacocks challenged her, even with a fine tipped marker. Her hands were itched to make those details in glass. The teal glass worked into the feathers should be breathtaking. If she had the glass.

The thought echoed in her mind, rolling around, getting louder until it hit her stomach. Where could it be, anyway? She had to find out who signed for the delivery and where it was because reordering it wasn't possible.

The jarring ring of the phone startled her. She punched the talk button. "Hello?"

"Hi, Deni."

"Lori! I thought you weren't going to call until Wednesday."

"I couldn't stand it. I miss talking to you, friend. Besides, I had to know how things are going. Tell me everything."

"It's been nice. Hot, but nice. I guess you want more details than that."

"Of course."

"We sailed out to an island where Joel played when he was little. It was primitive."

Lori groaned. "You didn't tell him that, did you?"

"Not exactly." She hesitated before continuing. "I left because I didn't like the sticker bushes."

"This is not the way to find your soul mate."

"If I have to trek through woods to find him, then you're right." Time to switch the top before Lori began her "Find a Mate," lecture. "Phase one of the back porch is finished."

"Phase one?"

"Joel gave me the plans and the cost. I can't afford it."

"What about the window? What are you going to do with it now?"

"That's phase two. Phase one contained the basics, steps, and a small porch."

"Isn't that going to be like what you had taken off?"

"It's a little bigger. Phase two happens when I make more money. Then I'll get to add on, making the floor larger, adding walls and then my window." Deni sighed. "Maybe by next summer I'll have enough money to finish."

"Tell me about the studio in town. Have you decided to rent it?"

"I love the building."

"I hear the uncertainty in your voice. So what's the problem?"

"I have to get a business plan, a license, a permit for the building, and I have to make sure the building will pass inspection before I sign the lease papers."

"That doesn't sound too hard. You've always excelled at filling papers."

"Only because I had to, Lori. I'd be rich if I could have been paid for filling out those stacks. They should have taught a class in college about the forms you have to fill out for special students. I can't believe

I thought it would end when I quit teaching. What if I rent this building, and no one signs up for classes? I'm just not sure this is the right plan."

"Why don't you stick with your original plan? Work out of the garage and then rent the building in the fall."

"I have to, but the realtor seemed to think the building won't be on the market long. By the time I have all I need it won't be there."

"And who always says to me, 'God will provide?'"

"I know I say it, and I believe it but — "

"You know He will provide what you need when you need it."

"I wish He'd provide me with my glass."

"It's still missing? You don't think someone would have taken it, do you?"

"Why would they want it?" Deni drummed her fingers on the worktable.

"Harder to stay in business making windows if you don't have materials to work with."

Chad wouldn't go that far, would he? At first, he'd made it clear that he wanted Joel to have the house. But lately, he'd been quiet about her moving and had been nice to her since their talk about Mandy.

What about Joel? Deni tried to push his face out of her mind. But try as she might, his image and his assurance that he would hold her forever attached themselves to a melody and played over and over in her mind.

CHAPTER THIRTEEN

Joel stepped inside the boathouse workshop, expecting to hear Chad tinkering with something. Silence greeted him. "Chad. You back there?"

"Up here, in the loft."

Joel walked to the stairs and looked up. Chad's head towered over a stack of boxes.

"Want me to come up?"

"Sure."

The worn wooden steps he climbed held indentations of footsteps of those in the past, including his. He'd spent his fair share of time working at the boathouse. A single bare bulb lit the center of the room, leaving the corners dressed in shadows. He blinked his eyes to adjust to the light. Boxes hugged the walls at odd angles.

"Why are you up here today? It's got to be close to a hundred degrees." He unbuttoned the top button on his shirt.

"Midyear inventory. Has to be done." With his foot, Chad shoved a cardboard box of oil filters to the side. He dragged the kerchief from his neck to his brow and wiped off the beaded sweat.

"Want some help?" Joel peeled off his suit coat.

"Nope. Don't have much left to do. Could use a break, though. Want to grab a soda? My treat."

"Sounds good. Are you coming down, or do you want me to bring it up here?"

"Just wait for me downstairs. I just have a couple of boxes to check." Chad pointed to the stack behind Joel.

He tossed his coat on a box near the steps. "I'll help, then we can both get out of this heat." He turned and bent to check the content label of the nearest box.

"Stop! I mean, I can do this myself. Besides, you have your pants to consider. You might get dust on them." Chad maneuvered between Joel and the boxes.

Chad scowled at him.

What did he do wrong now? "It's no problem. This suit needs to go to the cleaners. Anyway, I promised to help you do the inventory. I forgot, and you didn't remind me."

"I didn't think you'd have time since you're always with Deni." Chad moved closer to the box next to Joel. "I said, I'd take care of these."

"Don't be stubborn. I think the heat is getting to you." Joel opened box flap. He expected to see boxes of air filters and it took a second for his mind to register he was looking at sheets of glass.

Colored glass.

Deni's missing glass.

He stood, back stiff and hand clenched. "What are you doing with this?"

"Without it she can't work, right? Brings us closer to our dream. Remember our dream?"

"They don't always come true, and you have to find another way to achieve your goals. You know—a way that doesn't hurt someone." Right now he wouldn't mind causing his friend a bit of pain.

"She's not hurt."

"Listen to yourself. You sound like a kid. It does matter to her. She promised the church she'd do the window. She's also worried about not getting that first paycheck."

"Like I care? That's the reason I borrowed this." Chad kicked the box with his foot. "I'll take it over next week."

"No. I'll take it to her now." Joel bent over and picked it up. It was heavier than he expected. Climbing down the steps would be a challenge, but he wouldn't ask for help. "Don't do anything else to her. I don't want to have to choose between you. Right now, you would lose."

"It doesn't matter you've already chosen who matters."

"You both matter."

On the way to Deni's, Joel tried to think of a way to explain where he found it. Maybe if he could make her laugh about it? He drove past her driveway. He had to get something from his house before he told her.

🐐

Deni arranged the tools on top of the worktable. Tonight was her first class, she'd be working with kids again. Not little ones though. This would be different. The youth director called and asked her to teach the youth group a simple project.

She placed her cutter with the tungsten-carbide tool next to the ones the class would use. She wanted to show them the difference between them. They would use a cutter with a steel wheel which meant they would lubricate the wheel each time they scored the glass. Steel wheel cutters were difficult to use but cheaper to buy. Perfect for beginners.

Under each tool, she positioned printed cards for identification. She was sure "Fid" would get a laugh. Maybe she should write what the tool was used for to avoid explaining it is used to burnish the foil to the glass edges. Saying that ten times would make her think twice about teaching more than one class.

A knock on the garage door startled her. It was too early for the youth group to arrive.

"Deni, it's me."

She opened the door and found him wearing a red Santa hat.

"Surprise! I've brought you something you've been waiting for."

"You look silly in that hat. It's too early for Christmas, and I don't believe in Santa." Her heart beat fast.

"Do you believe in presents?" Joel bent down and whispered into her ear. "It's something you want maybe more than anything right now."

Deni's stomach fluttered in excitement. She wouldn't mind one of those kisses he'd been giving her.

"I do believe in presents."

"Close your eyes and wait right here."

Deni opened her eyes just a tiny bit then shut them fast when she realized he stared at her.

"Keep them closed."

"Now, can I open them?"

"Patience." His voice didn't sound close. He must have a real present for her.

Gravel crunched, and she inhaled his cologne. Yes, he was close to her now.

"Open your eyes."

A big cardboard box sat at her feet, Apelex Glass Company printed in the left-hand corner. "My glass! Joel! Where did you find it? I've been looking everywhere for it."

Before he answered, she reached up, pulled him close to her, and kissed him on the forehead.

"Thank you." She wrapped her arms around his neck, not wanting to let go. Not yet, it felt good to have him in her arms. She looked into his eyes. She wanted to kiss him again, only on the lips this time.

"Joel?"

"Um?"

"Would you, could you?" The rest of the question was lost as Joel bent down and caressed her lips with his.

"Is that what you wanted?" Joel smiled at her.

"Yes." She sighed, the warmth of the kiss sliding through her. "I mean, yes, the glass is perfect."

"Just the glass?"

"And the kiss. Where did you find the box?"

"In a place I least expected." Joel rubbed his chin with his hand. "I'm not sure I can explain how it ended up in Chad's storage loft."

"Chad had my glass all this time?" She pushed away from him and fisted her hands. Her fingernails dug into her palms. Her stomach churned. He didn't want her. "And you didn't know anything about it?"

"I didn't know he had it." He stroked her arm. "I knew you needed it, so I brought it right away."

"Sure you did. You had enough time to find that ridiculous hat first, didn't you?" Deni placed her hands on her hips. "Perhaps it was just another way to keep me from staying in this house."

🐐

Deni finger combed her hair, attempting to tame her unruly curls. The July humidity had made her curls twist and tighten in the July humidity. Her attempt ended without success.

Giving up, she gathered her hair in back, grabbed a gold clip and snapped it around her wild mane. Lori wouldn't expect her hair to be perfect anyway.

Too early to leave. She poured a glass of tea. Frosty tumbler in hand, she sat at the kitchen table. A hand-woven basket filled with bills rested in front of her.

"Eenie, meenie, miny moe-which bill am I going to...Hmm...To what...Pay tomorrow doesn't rhyme. Throw?" She rifled through the envelopes with her eyes closed and picked one. "Ugh, the real estate tax bill." She tossed it on to the table with a sigh. "I'll deal with that later."

There wasn't any way to avoid it. If she wanted to stay in this house, she would have to withdrawal money from the Guilt Fund

The Guilt Fund. Filled with blood money.

Lori always yelled at her when she said that, but she couldn't help how she felt. It was tainted, an attempt to replace something irreplaceable.

She dumped the ice from her glass into the sink then noticed the pets' water bowl was almost empty. She drained the stoneware dish and refilled it with fresh water.

Hershey's ears picked up the sound of tap water splashing in his bowl. He came, scooting round the corner.

"Here you go, Bud. Nothing quite like fresh water."

His ears hung over the sides of the bowl. He lapped the water then looked up at Deni as if to agree with her. Water dribbled from his mouth and puddled on the floor.

Shaking her head, she bent down with a dishcloth and wiped it up. She rubbed Hershey's ears. "Time to go, buddy. I'll be back in time to feed you." She grabbed her purse, scooped the car keys off the table and turned on the kitchen light.

She exited the door and stepped into nothing. Then felt her skin on her leg tear. She screamed in pain. Her vision narrowed into black nothingness.

She blinked. Why am I sleeping on the porch?

Hershey barked. The phone in her purse rang. She reached for it, but it was too far away. She tried to stand and then realized her left leg hung at a forty-five-degree angle from her right. Her other leg dangled through the broken porch boards. Her forehead stung. She rubbed it making it hurt more. Her hand now sticky and warm, covered with blood.

Hershey whined on the other side of the door.

She must have pulled it closed as she fell. "It's okay, boy. I'm okay." She pushed on the porch floor, trying to rise out of the hole. With a cry of frustration, she sank back. She wasn't strong enough to endure the pain radiating from her leg. "What am I going to do?"

Had the snakes returned to live under the porch? Goose bumps sprang out on her arms. Her will to get free renewed, she tried again. Would snakes be attracted to something moving, or was that sharks? Would it be better to stay still?

Her phone rang again. Tears stung her eyes. Help was a phone call away but not if the phone was out of her reach. She couldn't wait until someone happened along. It could be hours or even days before someone discovered her. No. It couldn't be days, could it?

She tried to remember when Chad was supposed to come back and work. He would bring Doug. She promised to help him make a night light. When was that? Tomorrow or the next day? She pounded the deck with her hand, and then she lay her head down and cried.

Her head ached from the pain of trying to reason her way out and from the physical pain of the split in her forehead. She couldn't stand it anymore. Desperation and fear dove deep into her mind sending a chill up her spine. Her phone rang again. "God, please! This is torture. If I could reach my purse." She stretched again. "It's useless. All the classes I've taken, I should be flexible enough to imitate a rubber band."

"Help! Anyone! Can anyone hear me on the lake?" She strained her ears listening for any response. None.

Hershey barked. Non-stop.

"Please, Hershey, stop. Please stop." She wiped the tears streaking her face. "Help! Can anyone hear me?" She yelled until her voice cracked. The phone rang again. If she ever got free, she was changing her ring   tone.

CHATPER FOURTEEN

Joel tightened his grip on the steering wheel. He had to find a way to get Deni to understand he had nothing to do with her missing glass. What a mess. What caused Chad to act this way? He had no idea, and right now he wasn't sure he cared enough to figure it out.

This afternoon he called Deni's phone at least twenty times, and it went to voice mail. She must still be furious with him. The green and white striped awning over Gator's Ice Cream Shoppe caught his eye. Maybe a peace offering would get him in her door. He whipped his car around, expertly parking it next to the curb.

Balancing two hot fudge sundaes and a small container of vanilla ice cream for Hershey in his left hand, Joel reached into his pocket for his keys. He pressed the key fob, the remote unlocked the car door. He settled the ice cream cups onto the passenger seat, adjusted all the air-conditioning vents toward them, and flipped the fan on high.

"Just thought I'd drop by. No, that sounds dumb." He grimaced as he drove over a bump in the dirt road.

He glanced at the ice cream. It remained upright. Grams would tell me to call again instead of surprising Deni.

Unbelievable. You would think he was actually afraid of that five-foot, four-inch ball of fire. He would let whatever rolled off his tongue be his opening line. Not like he had a choice. The house was right around the corner, and he hadn't come up with an original thought yet.

He parked and opened the door. Frenzied barking came from the house. Something was bothering Hershey.

"Help..."

Joel hesitated a second then turned back to the car. It sounded like . . . No, it had to be the wind.

"Please—"

That wasn't the wind. Something was wrong.

Hershey barked louder.

"Anyone out there?"

That scratchy voice sounded like Deni. Heart pounding, he ran for the house. "I'm coming!"

He bounded up the porch steps. He stared at Deni, half sprawled on the porch.

She wiped her eyes. "I'm so happy to see you."

He reached under her arms and pulled her from the hole. He held her close to him, his heart pounding in fear. "Are you hurt? How did this happen? When did this happen? How long have you been stuck?"

"I can only answer one question at a time."

"Are you hurt? Answer that one then." He held her away from him for a minute. "Yes. You are. You have a nasty cut on your head. Where are the house keys? I want to get you inside."

"By the door where I dropped them."

"Stay here. Can you lean against the wall?" Her keys clinked against the pewter heart when he picked them up. He opened the door. Hershey ran past him, straight for Deni.

"Off, boy. Don't jump. I'm okay." Deni patted him on the head.

Joel rubbed Hershey's ears. "It's okay, boy. I'll take care of her." He scooped her into his arms and stepped over the gaping hole in the porch into the kitchen. What it would be like to carry her over the threshold as his bride. The thought brought him immense pleasure.

"I think I can walk." As he carried her past the kitchen table, her dangling leg swiped a stack of papers onto the floor. She giggled. "Maybe I should try before we destroy my house."

Joel shifted her in his arms until her head rested against him and her hair brushed his chin.

"I'll put you down when I'm ready." She didn't weigh much. Did she conserve her money by not eating? He planned to check into that. Soon. He carried her through the kitchen into the living room. He placed her on the couch as if she were a precious antique.

"I suggest you rest here while I find a washcloth and antibiotic for your face and leg." Joel issued the order with a smile. He rushed to the bathroom, opened the medicine cabinet. It was so like Deni, the teacher. He shouldn't have been surprised she stocked it full of all sorts of first aid. She was ready for any emergency.

He came back carrying medical paraphernalia, "I can't believe I found a bottle of no-tears antibiotic spray."

"I'm not that brave."

Sitting on the couch next to her, he lifted her bangs as if they were strands of priceless glass that would shatter at the softest touch. Placing the washcloth on the broken skin he dabbed with a light touch. He sprayed the washcloth with the antibiotic and applied it to her skin.

"There now. That's done." He caressed the side of her face.

"You're good at that like you've had lots of practice."

"Someday I'll tell you about my medical experience." He knelt on the floor, picked up her foot and slipped off her shoe. "Now, we need to look at your leg and see what damage is done."

Her foot jerked out of his hand. "Stop it. I can take care of the rest of the damage. I'm not incapacitated."

"But I can — "Did her reaction have something to do with the reason she hid her leg more than wanting to prove she wasn't helpless?

"You know, I realized every time something goes wrong around here, you show up. Why is that? Do you want this house that much?"

"I don't know what-"

"You think I didn't notice while I was stuck on the porch for hours that a board had been removed? I'm lucky I didn't break my leg."

"What board? I didn't remove any boards." She sat tucked into the corner of the sofa like a scared kitten. What had he done to frighten her? Everything had been fine until he touched her shoe. Then she pulled her foot back faster than if she placed it in the jaws of a lion.

"Maybe you should leave. I can take care of myself."

"I brought ice cream."

"That doesn't make everything better, Joel."

The phone rang. Joel stood, uncertain about leaving. The phone rang again.

"That's probably Lori. I was supposed to meet her. You can let yourself out the back door. Oh and watch out for the hole in the porch." She reached into her purse and pulled out the phone.

"Call if you need me." He waited for an answer. She didn't even look at him. Would he ever find a way to make her trust him?

On his way through the kitchen, he bent down to pick up the scattered papers. He flipped through them and straightened them into a neat pile. On the top of the stack, he placed the real estate tax bill, then lay the pile the table. Should he go back and talk to her? He listened to her chatting on the phone. No, he'd come back later.

He hesitated before turning the back door knob. He rubbed his neck, then with a determined step, turned and grabbed the tax bill and shoved it into his pants pocket. If he paid it for her, maybe then she would understand how much he loved her.

He stood outside a moment, inspecting the damaged porch. No wonder she held him responsible for her fall. The missing board lay on the corner of the porch. Someone removed the nails and left them next to the board.

Deni watched through the window as Joel's car drove away. As the red taillights grew smaller, her heart squeezed tighter.

"Deni? Are you still there?" Lori's voice called to her from the phone.

"Yes. I was just watching Joel leave." She wished she could see his headlights coming back. She hated secrets but she couldn't share, not yet. She wasn't ready to say goodbye to him.

"So, you pretended to be mad because he wanted to bandage your leg? You've got to tell him why you reacted that way."

"No. I don't. Besides, how do I know that he didn't take that board out?"

"Do you really believe that?"

Deni sat on the couch, not saying anything. She knew in her heart that he didn't but if she were wrong...

"You can't be serious. You can't be thinking he would hurt you, risk breaking your arm or leg, just to get that house?"

"No. Maybe not. I guess not. I don't know what I think anymore. He was pretty aggressive at first about me leaving. If he didn't do it, then how did the board get removed?" Deni slid up her skirt and looked at her right leg. In the midst of purple-welted scars were bright red scratches and broken skin. "I'm tired. Can I call you back tomorrow?"

"Sure. We'll decide when to meet again. And Deni?"

"Yes?"

"If he loves you, he won't care what your leg looks like."

"I know. I'll talk to you later." She hung up the phone and whispered, "But will he care if I can't have children?"

Joel forced himself to back his foot off the accelerator. Punching it to the floor might get him to Chad's quicker, or it might send the car into something solid, like a tree—and he wanted to arrive at Chad's alive. Did he ever. He planned to talk to Chad in the morning, but after pacing his bedroom floor for the tenth time, he decided not to wait any longer.

He had plenty to say to him, even if he had to drag him out of bed. In fact, it would give him great pleasure to do just that. Why should he have the luxury of feeling safe in his house when he didn't want Deni to have that same comfort?

The car's tires had barely stopped spinning before Joel jumped out, slamming the door behind him. Marching up the steps ready to battle, his pulse raced.

He pounded on the door.

The door opened a crack. A small voice said, "Who's there?"

"It's me, Doug." What was he thinking? He'd forgotten about the little guy. He'd have to tone down his anger.

"Joel?" Doug rubbed his eyes. "It's dark outside. Why are you here?"

"I'm here to see your dad. Why are you opening the door, little man?"

"Dad let me sleep in my new sleeping bag on the floor and watch movies."

Chad stumbled into the living room. "Do you know what time it is?"

"I want to talk to you. Now. About Deni." Joel controlled his voice keeping the sharpness out of it for his godson's sake. "Get dressed and come outside."

Joel rubbed Doug's head. "See you later, bud. Go back to sleep in your new cocoon."

"It's a sleeping bag. And I'm not a butterfly."

Leaning against his car, Joel cracked his fingers. If he hadn't stopped by would she still be stuck, head bleeding and leg dangling? He clenched his jaw.

Light spilled into the dark as Chad stood in the open doorway. "I'll be back in a minute. Turn off the light and go to sleep, son." He closed the door behind him, leaving Joel in the darkness.

Joel's vision adjusted to the night sky. The quarter moon illuminated the driveway. Watching Chad approach, Joel found himself praying for the right words to say, words that wouldn't end a friendship but strengthen it. Words that would bring understanding to this madness.

"What's up? Didn't get me out of bed to look at the stars, did you?" He settled against the car next to Joel.

"Not exactly. What were you thinking?" His words came out sharp and clipped. Joel pushed off the car and faced Chad.

"About what?"

"Deni. What were you trying to do? Break her leg?" He grabbed Chad's arm.

"Is she okay?" Chad wrenched his arm out of Joel's grasp.

"She's pretty scratched up. She could have broken her leg. She hit her head. His voice caught, remembering Deni's frightened, tear-stained face. She was stuck in that hole for hours. She'd still be there if I hadn't decided to drop by with ice cream."

"Then if she's okay, what are you upset about? Is she ready to move?" Chad stuck his hands into the pockets of his jeans.

Joel took a deep breath and let it out slowly. "Do you know how much I'd like to stick you in a hole and leave you for a few days?"

"So much for being blood brothers. Do you remember? The night we cut our fingers and mixed our blood? We said we'd never betray each other." Chad spit the words out.

"I haven't. You betrayed me." Joel fisted his hands. He shoved them in his pockets to keep them from flying loose on Chad. "I told you I loved her. I'm going to marry her if you don't kill her first."

"I'm not going to kill her. Don't be stupid."

"You won't for the very reason you mentioned. We're blood brothers. We promised to always be there for each other. I've been here for you, and now I need you to be here for me." Joel's head throbbed. "Why is this so difficult? We can find another place to build the resort."

"You like her that much?" Chad scuffed his feet in the gravel drive.

"I love her. Why don't you understand?" Joel put his hand on Chad's shoulder. "What's gotten into you? Tell me why I shouldn't deck you for what you've done?"

Chad shoved Joel away. "I'd like to have something go right for once. I've dreamed of that resort for years. I don't want anything or anyone to stop the plans we made together.

"And I don't want you to end up like me. I'm trying to protect you, blood brother. I don't want you to know the pain of rolling over in bed and feeling nothing. Or waking up in the middle of the night because you thought you heard someone whisper, 'I love you." Chad walked back to his house and then turned before he went inside. "Just forget it, okay? I'll leave both of you alone. Neither of you has to worry anymore."

CHAPTER FIFTEEN

Hammering interrupted Deni's sleep. Confused, she forced open her eyes. Pink gauze from the early dawn danced across her room. The sun wasn't up yet.

Groggy from changing positions all night while trying to find a painless way to lay, she thought it might be Chad working. But it was Saturday. He would be busy at the boat shop with weekend boaters. If it wasn't Chad, then who was it?

She groaned as she placed weight on her injured leg. Her entire body throbbed. Her right leg was stiff, but she forced herself to hobble to the window. Looking down, she spotted Joel's car. The noise had to be coming from him.

She winced as she slipped on a pair of jeans and a pink T-shirt. As she raised her arm to brush her teeth, she moaned. She worked hard to get herself out of that hole yesterday, and her body reminded her.

Walking down the stairs her leg cramped. She sat on the middle step and rubbed her shin. She was tired. Maybe she should give up and move back to Missouri. She could work at the mall or some hamburger joint until she found a teaching position next year.

"Father, what should I do? Am I being stubborn? Or do You want me to stay here and use the gift of creativity You gave me? I need to know God because right now leaving this place seems like the logical thing to do." The hammer struck again. Would Joel be out there this early in the morning if he removed the board in the first place? Maybe, if guilt pricked him. Or if Chad took it out, and Joel wanted to make things right.

She stood, ready to apologize to Joel. By the time she reached the bottom step, her body tensed. If Joel cared anything about her, why didn't he protect her from his friend? Or maybe they were in it together, a sort of good cop/bad cop thing?

Marmalade threaded her body around and through Deni's legs, meowing her morning greeting. Hershey sat by the back door, whining and thumping his tail.

"Morning, Hersh. You want out to say hi to Joel?"

Hershey's tail beat faster on the floor, and he gave a small yelp.

"Out you go, then." Deni unlocked the door and let Hershey free. He pummeled Joel and licked his face. Traitor.

"You didn't need to fix my porch. I could have done it myself later this morning. After all, it is Saturday. I know you have plans."

"Morning to you, too. Sorry, I woke you, but I wanted to do this before anyone else gets hurt."

"Thanks, but I could have managed to slam in a few nails after breakfast."

"I just thought you might be too sore to get on your hands and knees. How are you feeling this morning?"

"I'm hurt all over." Deni gathered her courage, remembering what Lori said about telling Joel the truth. It might be easier if those brown eyes of his didn't make her want to be loved. "About last night."

"Don't want to talk about it. You were hurt and scared." He put the hammer down, rested his hands on top of her shoulders. "I would never hurt you."

"Are you saying I can stop wondering if you are still trying to get this house? My home?"

"Are you always a tiger in the morning?" He backed away from her, pretending to cower.

Deni's lips tipped up into a grin. "Only if I'm awakened by harsh sounds."

"Would you prefer being awakened with a kiss?"

She snorted. "I am not somebody's princess. Never will be."

"How do you know?"

"I just do, so let's leave it at that. How much do I owe you for fixing my porch?"

"Make me dinner tonight?"

"I can do that, but will it be eatable?" She grinned. "Be here by six, or you don't eat."

She stepped back into the kitchen.

He called through the closing door. "I'll be seeing you later, Princess."

Joel waited in front of the drugstore for Colin's mother to arrive. He should have told Deni about Chad's reason for his behavior. She would have understood, he was certain. He'd tell her tonight what Chad had said about missing Mandy.

Shelly walked down the street carrying Colin. He knew he'd need to explain to Deni soon about how he spent his Saturday mornings playing with the cutest two-year-old in town. Maybe next Saturday, she could come too. They could take Colin to the St. Louis Zoo.

"Hi, Shelly. Here. Let me take him from you."

Colin giggled and reached for Joel's nose.

"He gets heavier every week." Joel kissed the child on the forehead.

"I wouldn't be surprised if he is. He's like his father, eating all the time." Shelly grimaced. "I hope he doesn't turn out like him too."

"Not a chance with you as a mom. I'll bring him back to your house, fed and tired at about one, okay?" Joel enjoyed the way the toddler felt in his arms. He hoped to have a large family someday. Did Deni want a big family too?

Deni almost missed seeing Joel on the sidewalk. Her mind was occupied with making a list of what items she needed to buy for the evening meal. At least, she thought it was him. But why would he be holding a little boy? And who was that woman with him?

Twisting to the left for a better look she watched the woman kiss Joel on the cheek. Her Joel.

Fuming inside, Deni glanced back to the street in front of her. In horror, she saw the bright red brake lights of the car up ahead. Visions of the accident flew into her head. She stomped her foot on the brake.

She gasped for air. Hands shaking from the near miss, she managed to drive to the grocery store.

Safe in a parking space, she lay her head on the steering wheel. Her stomach ached, and her heart pounded as if she'd danced for hours without resting.

Had Joel had witnessed her poor driving? Angry for even caring, she flung open the car door. The sweltering heat bouncing off the blacktop parking lot reminded her of Joel's kisses. He was making her crazy.

"I am such a fool." It had to be a trick, a ploy to get her land. Joel didn't love her. Not if he was kissed another woman. Did the child belong to him? She was right from the beginning. He couldn't be trusted.

Better the devil known than unknown, as her grandmother used to say. Dinner would continue as planned, with a small change in ingredients. Hot peppers and Italian sausage. Keeping Joel awake with a little indigestion would bring a tiny touch of satisfaction in the early hours before dawn.

An hour before Joel was to arrive for dinner, Deni stacked photo albums on the top of the coffee table. They held dance recital pictures and the last one filled with recovery pictures.

With a lead-heavy heart, she flipped through the pages. She rubbed her leg at an imaginary throbbing.

"Those will send him running, just like Rob. I won't even cry when he stutters out an excuse about having to leave." She flopped onto the couch.

Marmalade stretched, arching her back. With a small meow, she jumped from her place on the rocker to the couch. She kneaded Deni's chest before settling down with a soft purr.

"Ach, I'm kidding myself, Marmy. Losing Joel hurts." She closed her eyes and rubbed the soft fur on Marmalade's head. "I don't understand. Why do You want me to live alone, God?"

CHAPTER SIXTEEN

Standing on Deni's porch, Joel heard Deni talking through the open window.

"No Rob, I don't think so."

Rob? That was her ex-fiancé, wasn't it? What did he want?

"Fine, I'll pray about it. Maybe trying again would work. But I'm not giving you my answer yet. Later."

Joel waited for a second before knocking on the door. He didn't like the overheard words. She couldn't be thinking about getting back together with Rob. He'd have to change her mind. He would never lose something this right, this important to him not without a fight.

Deni stood before him in the open doorway. Her hair curled around her face made her look angelic. He touched the tip of her nose.

"I've missed you. You've been in the sun. I see two new freckles." Joel encircled her.

Deni pushed away from him, surprising him. "I need to check on dinner."

Her words sounded scissor sharp. He didn't think he did anything wrong by kissing her. Maybe Rob's phone call upset her.

Joel followed her into the kitchen. "Smells terrific."

"I hope you don't mind spicy food." She smiled at him. "It should be done in about twenty minutes."

"Good, because I want to talk to you."

"Let's get something cool to drink and sit in the living room. I have something to tell you too."

He touched her shoulder. "I'd like to sit on the beach. We should have enough time."

Hershey ran ahead of them as they walked to the lake. They watched him run into the water, bite the waves, and run back to the sand.

"What did you want to tell me?"

"I wanted to tell you about my Saturday mornings and how I spend them."

"You don't have to."

"I want to. You're a part of my life, and you need to know what I do. I wanted to go to college to be an architect. You know that part already. What you don't know is there wasn't money for me to go to school. So I made a deal with God. I told Him if I get my degree, I would find a way to pay Him back."

"God doesn't make deals."

"Let me finish. One day, I opened my mail and discovered a foundation chose me for a full scholarship. I knew then God had accepted my deal. Don't shake your head. It's true. Listen to the rest, okay?"

"All right, I'll listen, but then it's my turn, okay?"

"I will. I promise. After I had graduated, I found a way to help God. I signed up with the Big Brothers Association. Every Saturday morning, I pick up a child and do something with him. I just started with a new family about a month ago. Shelly's a single mother. She works on Saturday mornings, and I take her two-year-old son, Colin to the park to play."

"Big Brothers," Deni repeated in a monotone voice.

Joel stopped walking and turned to look at her face. Something didn't seem right.

"Deni?"

"I'm sorry, Joel. I didn't know."

"Why should you be sorry? You couldn't have known because I hadn't told you."

"Because, because." Deni's voice quivered. "I saw her kiss you. I thought — "

"You thought I was seeing someone else? Deni, you are the only woman in my life since you moved into the house. The only person I want in my life, forever, is you."

195

"Forever?"

"Would you marry me?" Joel tilted her chin and placed a kiss on her lips.

She wanted to scream yes and wrap her arms around him. "I would like to. But I have to talk to you about something first."

"Joel, Deni? Are you on the beach?" Chad's voice echoed in the air.

"Why is he here?" Joel yelled, "Just wait. We're on our way back."

Chad sat on the porch steps rubbing Hershey's damp head. "Good smells are coming from your kitchen, Deni."

"It's a spicy dish." She cringed inside, thinking about the ingredients she used.

"I like spicy foods. Do you think I could eat with you two? I need to talk to both of you."

She gave Joel a quick glance. "I suppose it would be all right."

"Do you have enough?" Joel asked.

"More than enough." Again, guilt tugged at her heart. No one would be able to eat much of her revenge dinner.

🐕

Deni sat next to Joel on the couch. The photo albums on the table mocked her as Joel reached over to pick one up. Not wanting to talk about her past in front of Chad, she scooped up the books and set them on the end table.

"I don't want to get distracted while Chad talks." And she didn't want to share her past with anyone but Joel.

Chad sat, shoulders slumped and stared at his hands. "This is so hard."

"It's okay, Chad. We're listening." Joel leaned back on the couch and rested his arm around Deni's shoulders.

"I want to start by saying I'm sorry to you and Deni." Chad straightened in the overstuffed chair. "Deni, I didn't mean for you to get hurt falling into the hole in the porch."

"I could have broken my leg." Deni nails bit into her palms.

"I know. I wanted to scare you into leaving, to get you to move back where you came from."

"What did I do to you that you dislike me that much?" She turned to Joel. "Did you know about this?"

"Yes. I planned to tell you everything tonight."

"Everything?" Deni stared at Chad in disbelief. "What else is there?"

"I put the snakes in the kitchen and intercepted the glass from the delivery person. Joel didn't do anything to harm you. It was me."

"Why would you do such a thing?" Deni wanted to scream at him. The terror he put her through with those snakes, how she'd lain awake at night worried more might get inside.

"At first, I thought it was because I wanted Joel to get the land. It was a boyhood dream of ours." Chad hunched over as if he aged in the last five minutes. "But then, it was something more. After Joel came to see me, I realized I didn't want him to suffer like I have. And I didn't want to lose him. He's my only friend since Mandy. We had plans. You spoiled them."

Her anger gave way to understanding. "I want you to know that I forgive you, but what you did was wrong."

"I know. That's why I'm going to go into grief counseling. I went this afternoon, and I think it might help. If you want to press charges against me for harassment, I'll understand." Chad pulled his hands away from Deni's and stood. "I'm going home. Please call if you are going to contact the police so I can warn Doug first."

Stunned, she sat in silence and watched him leave.

"Deni?" Joel's warm voice had a concerned tone. "I hate to leave you, but I need to make sure he gets home safe. I owe that to Doug and Mandy."

"Go, please. Tell him as long as he stays in counseling, I won't go to the police." She leaned over and brushed through his hair.

"I'll call you in the morning." He gave her a quick kiss goodbye.

It wasn't until she picked up the tray of empty glasses that she realized she hadn't given Joel an answer to his proposal. She relished that, for a little while, he wanted to marry her. That would all change when he saw the photos and heard her story.

🐐

With the early morning sun peeking through dusty blue clouds, Deni dressed for church. She didn't wait for Joel to call. She needed to talk to God, and Lori. God, she could talk to anywhere. But Lori was in Missouri, so that's where she would go.

During the first hymn, she slipped into her old comfortable pew next to Lori. She sat, fidgeting with the bracelet on her arm and changing the position of her legs. During the sermon, Lori shot her looks like a mother uses on a small child. She tried to stay still but found herself tapping the hymnal cover.

As soon as the pastor gave the blessing and went to the door to greet the congregation, Lori placed her hymnal in the rack and faced Deni.

"Let's have it," Lori demanded. "Why are you here?"

"I wanted to visit." Her voice squeaked.

"I know better than that. Just what or who are you running from?"

"You're terrifying. Did you know that?" Deni glared at Lori.

"I've known you a long time. There's only one solution for what's bothering you. Let's go to Pancake World and talk."

"What would I do without your friendship? Fluffy pancakes are just what I need to feel better." Deni moaned. "Chocolate-chip-laden cakes served with hot chocolate sauce and fluffy whipped cream will take care of any problem. Let's go."

Once inside the restaurant, Deni spotted a lone unoccupied booth in the corner. She slid across the crackling green vinyl seat. Lori sat across from her. Both remained silent while looking over the pancake specialties.

"I'm sticking with my original order." Deni slid the menu behind a plastic cow creamer.

"Brown sugar and cinnamon sound perfect to me. I could eat here every morning."

After the waitress had left with their order, Lori said, "Tell me everything. Don't leave out one thing."

Glancing around the crowded diner, Deni leaned over and whispered, "Joel asked me to marry him."

"Hallelujah! You did say yes, didn't you?" Lori squealed and clapped.

"Lori! Not so loud." Where people staring? She didn't want to look.

"Well, it was a yes, wasn't it?"

"No. I mean, I didn't give him an answer."

"Why not?"

"Because Chad came over last night while Joel was there. I planned to tell him about my accident, but then Chad showed up and stayed for dinner." She told Lori what she made for dinner and why.

Lori laughed. "That was pure meanness, but your grandmother would have been proud of you if you hadn't jumped to conclusions. You are lucky they didn't get sick."

"I know. If I confronted Joel with what I saw, I wouldn't have had to serve so much ice water. But Chad had a reason for being there."

"Not a good one, from the look on your face."

"He's the one responsible for all the things happening at the house. The snakes, the hole in the porch, my missing glass."

The waitress slid their breakfast plates on to the table.

"Why would Chad do that?"

"He wanted me to move. He said he was protecting Joel from being hurt the way he was when his wife died. He wanted Joel to have the house so they could build their resort together. He was being selfish."

"Oh, that is so sad. He must have loved her completely. Wouldn't it be wonderful to be loved that way?"

"Yes, it would, and you will be someday. God just hasn't shown you the one yet."

"I think Joel will love you like that. You are going to tell him yes, right?"

"He hasn't met all the requirements on my list yet."

"Throw the list away. You don't need it for this guy. He's nothing like Rob." Lori stabbed a pancake-laden fork at her. "Besides, he met the important items on the list."

"But not all of them." Deni cut her pancakes into tiny pieces. "I still have to tell him about Lane."

CHAPTER SEVENTEEN

Joel and Chad sat on the deck outside of Chad's kitchen with steaming coffee cups in their hands. Chad bounced his leg. "Better switch legs. The way you're moving that one, it'll have more muscles than the other one."

"I'm in trouble." Chad stopped moving. "Financially. I don't know how things got so bad. I owe two months' rent on this dump, and I'm supposed to make it into a home for Doug. I can't afford to move. The electric company gave me two weeks until they cut off the power."

"I knew—hoped that if we opened the resort I could get back on my feet. Maybe start over in a smaller house where Doug could have a yard to play. Maybe even get a dog." Dark half-circles hung under Chad's eyes.

Why hadn't Joel noticed before? "How did it get this bad? Why didn't you ask for help?"

"Medical bills." Chad drained his coffee cup. "They just kept coming. They're still coming. And funeral bills. I had no idea it was so expensive to die. We didn't have life insurance, you know that. We thought there'd be plenty of time to get it. And then it was too late."

"And you didn't ask for help because...?"

"I don't want charity."

"So, the real reason you wanted Deni gone was because of money."

"Yes, and no. You're my best friend, and I guess I was jealous of the time you spent with her. I know that sounds weird, but we've hung out a lot this past year. And that's helped the loneliness." Chad blinked. "And she reminds me of Mandy. Not in looks, but the soft way she glances at you or touches your arm. That hurts. Hurts bad."

"Last night I asked her to marry me."

"When's the wedding?" Chad spoke without expression.

"Don't know." Joel rubbed the rough stubble on his chin. "I just asked her when you yelled for us. I didn't get an answer."

"What do you think she'll say?" Chad slapped a mosquito. "I hope I haven't messed things up for the two of you."

"I don't know if she'll say yes. I heard her talking to her ex-fiancé. Sounds like he wants to get back together."

"Is that why you asked her last night?"

"Thought I'd better not waste any more time."

"Don't let her get away. The love and care a good wife gives to you is a treasure you can't find anywhere. Better try calling her again."

Stiff from sleeping on Chad's sofa, Joel stretched an arm over his head as he listened to the hollow sound of the phone ringing. He knew Deni should be back from church by now. Maybe she forgot to turn it back on.

"She's still not answering."

"I told you to meet her this morning. I'm fine."

"We've already been through this. I didn't want to leave until I felt you were okay. She'll understand. She's had a lot of pain in her life, too."

"I didn't know that. Guess I've been too busy focusing on my own grief."

Doug came outside.

"Hey, sleepy head." Joel grabbed him as he walked by, pulling into a hug. "Don't you talk in the morning?"

Through eyes opened just enough to see, Doug peered at him. "What's for breakfast? Can we have eggs?"

Chad laughed. "That's my boy. Food before hospitality."

"What's pospitaly?" Doug asked.

"That's when you say hi before placing your breakfast order." Joel smiled.

"Like the man that lives in the speaker at McDonald's? He says good morning before we tell him we want pancakes and sausage."

"Munchkin, I'll make you scrambled eggs unless your dad wants to impress you with his culinary skills."

"Dad, don't make culinary. It doesn't sound good." Doug wrinkled his nose.

Joel picked the boy up and held him over his head. "Green stuff makes you strong, like your dad and me."

Doug squealed with laugher as Joel turned in circles. "I'm flying." He imitated a plane.

"Time to land the bird," Chad said. "Run and get dressed while Joel and I get breakfast on the table."

"Okay." Doug stretched out his arms like wings and flew into the house.

"Try calling her one more time." Chad pulled the egg carton off the refrigerator shelf.

Joel wanted to talk to Deni. He needed to know the answer to his question, and the unanswered phone didn't offer him any comfort.

While driving down the gravel road to Joel's house, Deni glanced at the photo albums on the seat next to her. Lori suggested meeting Joel at his house. Then she could be the one to leave if he acted like Rob, though Lori insisted Joel wouldn't be anything like her ex-fiancé.

Deni's stomach twinged. "Father, please don't let him be like Rob. At least let him be kind."

Holding her photos close to her chest, she knocked on his door. Her heart fluttered, and her mind told her to run while she still had her dignity.

Joel opened the door, a look of surprise and longing on his face. "Hi, Princess." He pulled her close and hugged her tight. "I've been trying to call. I'm glad you're here, and you're all right. I was worried about you."

"I forgot to turn my phone back on. I'm sorry." His words gave her the courage to continue with her plan. "I brought pictures to show you."

"But first, are you going to answer my question?"

"Not until I talk to you about my past." She wanted his unconditional love so much she ached. She followed him into the living room. Still clutching the photo albums, she sat in a chair facing the couch.

"I'm guessing you want me to look at some pictures. How am I supposed to do that if you're over there?" He patted the sofa next to him. "Come over here and stop worrying."

Trying to settle her nerves, she took a breath deep enough to find the center of the earth, then exhaled. She sat next to him and closed her eyes, then offered a quick request for the right words to say.

"Deni?" Joel's soft voice interrupted what was beginning to be a long monologue to God.

"Sorry. I'm afraid."

"I know." Joel clasped her hand in his. "There is nothing you can say, or show me, that will keep me from loving you. I don't even have to see these pictures."

"No. Yes. I mean, you have to look at them. We have to start our marriage with honesty."

"Then you will marry me?" Joel smiled at her.

"Maybe." She slowly withdrew her hand from his. "When I was sixteen, I had a dance contest in Chicago. My grandmother wanted me to fly or take the train. I wanted to drive. I badgered her until she gave in and let me. My dance partner, Lane, rode with me. Dance was everything to me. I went to class every night, I taught classes, and I'd won many competitions. I thought someday I'd be able to join a professional dance company."

"Are these dance pictures?"

"Some of them, yes." She handed him the top album. "These are my recital pictures."

She watched Joel's face as he flipped through the pages. He stopped to study one photo.

"That's my favorite. I played Clara in The Nutcracker Suite at the Fox Theater that year. I was fifteen."

"You had to be good to get that part."

"I was. God gave me the gift of balance and grace. But then..." The lump in her throat swelled. "I had an accident."

"What happened?"

"Joel." She hesitated, hoping the next words she said wouldn't come out wrong. "Please...This is difficult for me. Could you listen to the whole story without interruptions?"

"It may be hard not to stop you, but I'll try."

"Rain slicked the roads. The windows fogged. Lane slept in the passenger seat. I had trouble seeing. I didn't want to wake him up to stop the car and wipe the windows." She bit her lip to keep from crying. "Headlights shone into my car. I veered to the right. The car hit us. Lane went through the windshield. He didn't have his seat belt on correctly. He died on the way to the hospital."

"Were you hurt? Sorry, I'll be quiet."

"Yes. I had pilot fractures in both legs. I must have tried to stop the car with both feet. The impact pushed my ankles into my shins. They put me back together

209

with pins, which left ugly scars. I had to learn to walk again." She whispered.

"I don't care if you have a body full of scars. I love you, the Deni inside, and the Deni I see before me. I love the way you close your eyes and whisper a prayer any time you want. The way..."

"Shh, Joel, there's more." She couldn't help it. The tears poured forth. "The steering wheel went into my stomach. I had internal bleeding, too. The surgeons repaired it, but now I can't have children. Ever." Deni covered her eyes and sobbed. "I know you want kids. You'll make a good father. That's why I can't marry you."

The sofa cushion moved as Joel stood up. This is it. Now, he'll tell me he wants to remain friends. He surprised her by touching her chin, raising her head so she looked at him. He stood before her.

He got down on his knees before her, "Deni, please marry me. Yes, I want kids. Yes, I want you to be their mother, collecting handprints in made of plaster of Paris on Mother's Day."

"But?"

"We can adopt as many children as you want."

Deni remained silent, sitting in disbelief.

"Think about it. Children of your own are important. I can't give you those."

"There are lots of ways to be a parent. We can adopt. It will be okay."

She stared at him, thanking God. She thanked Him for giving her a man of understanding. She thanked Him for a man that wanted to adopt. She thanked Him for giving her a Christian man. She thanked Him for Lori's urging her to talk to him.

"Um, Deni, if you're done talking to God would you tell me if we should start planning a wedding?"

With a lightened heart, she checked to see if her feet were still touching the ground. "Just one more question. Do you like cotton candy?"

"Only if it's pink."

She sighed with satisfaction.

"Will you tell me something about the window? I've been working on the puzzle of the three birds. I can't come up with an association. I've figured out the plane was your parents, the ballet shoes were for dance, but those birds. I can't figure those out."

"It's easy. I'll give you a hint."

"No, the answer. I'm telling you, I'm worn out thinking about it."

"Three birds. The three is significant."

"Deni."

"They stand for the Trinity."

"Of course. Why didn't I think of that? The Father, Son, and Holy Spirit. You're clever." Joel hugged her and whispered in her ear, "Are you going to say yes to my question? Will you marry me?"

"Yes, I'll marry you. But where are we going to live?"

"I knew you would ask that. Let's discuss it over dinner tomorrow night."

"I don't know if I can wait that long. What about breakfast or lunch?"

"No, I want to take you to dinner at Andria's and show you off to the world, because you're my princess."

His princess. For the first time in forever she believed she could be one.

***

Joel drove the noisy, rusty truck down Deni's drive. He was unsure what her reaction would be when he told her what he did with his car.

Hershey approached the truck with teeth bared. Joel hoped Deni would smile at least.

"Hey, Hersh." Joel stepped out of the door. "Off, boy, you're getting me dirty, and this is a special night for your mom." She waited on the porch, beautiful in an ankle-length navy-blue sheath.

"Where's your car?" Deni looked past him.

"That's something I need to talk to you about. Climb on in, and I'll tell you everything on the trip to town."

He opened the passenger door for her and grimaced at the loud screech. "It needs a little work."

She raised her eyebrows in a question.

"Okay, more than a little." With her safe inside, he slammed the creaky door. Once he was inside he pulled a velvet box out of his pocket and handed it to her.

"Open it. Now, please."

She lifted the lid to reveal a simple gold band. "A wedding ring?"

"Yours. I know it should be an engagement ring, but that will come later. Read the inscription on the inside."

Deni peered into the delicate ring, tilting it into the light. "A time to dance?"

"Lori told me your grandmother gave you the key chain when she wanted you to go on with life."

"She wanted me to realize that a time to dance" means a time to act because dancing is motion. It's not standing still. I had to go on with my life. But why are you saying it to me?"

"I want you to think about what your grandmother told you. Don't say anything until I finish. Just like the other night when I had to be still and listen."

"If I remember, I had to remind you to be still. Go ahead. I'll be quiet."

"First," he handed her an envelope. "Open this."

Peeling back the paper, Deni pulled out a receipt. "You paid my taxes?"

"Shh. Remember, you said you wouldn't talk. I paid the taxes. We're getting married. Which means the house will be mine too. Stop glaring at me. I didn't propose just to get it." He leaned over and kissed her forehead. "Don't panic."

"Where are we going to live?"

"A reasonable question. I like the idea of living in my house. It's bigger, and it has more bedrooms for those children we plan to have." Deni's face flushed. He decided he'd better tell her the rest of it fast or the wedding invitations would never be ordered.

"But are you listening? This is important. The lake house isn't going to be torn down or made into a resort. Ever."

"But what...sorry." Deni pretended to zip her lips.

"I think that if it's okay with you we should let Chad and Doug move in rent-free until he can get back on his feet financially. He can continue to fix the place up instead of paying rent money he doesn't have. If that's okay with you. After Chad can make it on his own and moves out, I thought we might continue to offer the house at a reduced rent to another family in need."

"Joel, I love you. Wait, you aren't doing this as part of the deal with God, are you?"

"No. God doesn't make deals, remember? I'm doing it because God blessed me with so many gifts, and I want to give it back to others in His name."

"That's wonderful!"

"Now, about the truck. I sold my car to pay the taxes and to put a deposit on this place." He stopped the truck in front of the building Deni wanted for her studio. "It's only right you have a place to work since the garage at the lake house will be used by someone else."

She stood with her mouth open.

"This is your engagement ring." He held out a key ring with a set of keys. "Want to try it on?"

"It's beautiful! I love the stone you've chosen. Old brick. Not many can say they have a ring like this one." She hugged him and whispered in his ear. "Thank you. I'm glad God taught me to trust you."

She opened the door to her new studio. Sunlight streaked through the window onto the wooden floor. She turned to him, bowed, and walked to the center of the room. Humming she swayed, then spun, holding her hand toward him. "Dance with me, please, for the rest of our lives."

He walked to her and took her hand. "Forever."

EPILOGUE

Deni held the photo of her parents on their wedding day. She wanted to carry it down the aisle but how? "Have any idea Lori?"

"Let's see, the dress doesn't have pockets." She took the photo from Deni. "It's amazing how much you look like your mom, and you found someone to make a similar dress."

"Thankfully, Mom liked things simple and chose a simple A-line in satin." She smoothed the dress. "I think the gloves were a bit too much for me even if they looked good on my mom."

"Hershey would carry one off before you got them both on, anyway." Lori stuck the photo in the middle of the bridal bouquet. "There what do you think about that?"

"Perfect. I wouldn't have considered doing that. It doesn't stick out, and the greenery hides it from the sides. I'm doing this for me not to get the guests all emotional."

"It's going to be anyway, but I do understand. It's just different for me."

"I'm praying for you. That you'll have courage to call home."

"Today is about you not me, okay?"

"Fine, but I'm not giving up on a Peterson reunion. I'd love to meet them someday."

"Do you think Hershey's going to behave?" Lori picked up her camera and snapped a photo.

"I hope so. Joel has been training him every day. He knows there will be a treat when he gets next to Joel's dress shoes and that he's to sit and stay until he is released. It might be crazy to have him in the wedding, but when Joel suggested it, I got this warm feeling all over like it was meant to be." Right now she wished Hershey were with her, helping her get ready, but Joel had taken him for the day suggesting she might be less wrinkled without Hershey's help.

"Stand by the window and put the flowers near your face. This needs to be documented on all of my social media sites. You're so beautiful. Joel makes you happy it's easy to see. Someday-"

Deni's dress rustled as she positioned herself. "It's going to happen for you. I know it, Lori. God has a plan."

"I know, but I wish he'd implement it sooner than later." She took several photos. "Those are nice. I'm not a professional, but I'd like to be."

"Maybe you should go back to school and learn what you need to be a professional?"

"Yeah, I might, but right now my job is to get you to the church so you can marry the man who made the list."

"Let's go then. I can't wait to hear Mr. and Mrs. Joel Anderson."

🐐

Deni peaked out of Joel's kitchen window, now hers too. She and Joel had decided to have the reception here. The caterers set up a white tent on the beach for the dinner. Two striped changing tents were nearby where a guest could switch from formal clothes to beachwear. Inflatable rings of many colors dotted the shoreline making Deni smile at the wedding gift from Chad and Doug, who probably influenced his father on the present choice.

She backed away from the window and slipped her heels off and sighing with relief slid into her flip flops. The wedding was everything Deni had ever dreamed of, and everything she hadn't. The dress fit perfectly, her hair didn't frizz, and her groom had been picked by God, of that she was certain. But there was a hole in her heart, and it hurt. She sniffled.

"What's wrong?" He stroked her cheek. "Did I do something to upset you already?"

"No. You've been wonderful even letting Hershey carry the rings down the aisle. It's just I wish my dad could have walked me down the aisle and mom could have shopped for my dress with me."

"It's okay to miss them." Joel wiped a tear from her eye. "Your mom and dad should be here, you should have brothers and sisters threatening my life if I don't take care of you, and your grandmother should have been here."

Deni nodded and swallowed back a sob. He knew and understood so well.

"Look out there at all the people who are here that love you. You don't have friends you have so much more than that. They are your family."

"I know. I'm blessed to have them."

"You have my family too. They don't all know you as well as your friends but give them time. They want to be your family."

"Your sister told me. Actually, she said if you don't behave, let her know and she'd take you out. She touched his arm. "I think she meant it."

"I'm sure she did. I promise to never be bad enough to invoke her form or torture."

"Before we greet our guests, I want to talk to you about the Guilt Fund." She sniffed.

"There's no need, sweetheart. I will stand by your decision not to spend it."

"No, I think I'm wasting a precious resource. Could you design some small houses that would rent at a small price for single mothers or fathers? It would be special for them to have a place on the lake." She stepped away and watched his face. His looked over her head, pursed his lips.

"I will agree as long as we rename the money."

"No more Guilt Fund?" She'd been saying that so many years. It felt right to let it go. But what would they call it?

"How about the Second Chance at Hope Fund?"

Deni squealed. "I love it! Let's do it and let's tell Chad today that he gets to help in some way."

"Did I ever tell you that you're the best wife I could ever have?

"Not yet, but I hope you tell me that every day." She reached for him, and he drew her into a hug.

We've come to the end of Deni and Joel's story but what about Chad?

Will Chad continue on his journey of recovery and turn his life around? Will he become a role model Doug?

Can Chad ever fall in love? Because if he does, he's going to have to tell her about this ugly episode in his life.

Find out more in <u>A Time to Bake. Get it now!</u>

Or page through to read the first chapter.

Back of the Book Notes,

Dear Reader,

Thank you for reading A Time to Dance. I so appreciate you. There was a time in my adult life that taking a ballet class gave me back my self-esteem and a little grace. When you are forced to know where your body is at any moment your mind stops thinking about the what ifs? and why did? scenarios in your brain. Could this be what God meant by the verse in

Ecclesiastes A time to dance? Maybe, though I'm not a biblical scholar so you'll have to ask one.

If you enjoyed this story, please consider leaving a review. Please make sure you're on my newsletter mailing list at dianabrandmeyer.com to keep up with the latest news about my books. And find me on Facebook where I get cozy with my readers.

As always, thank you to my husband Ed Brandmeyer, and those who support me behind the scenes, Jennifer Crosswhite, Liz Tolsma and Angela Breidenbach. I couldn't do this without all of you.

Thank you! Because of you I can write the stories God gives me to share. I am so grateful to each of you. Keep reading for a look at my next book.

In His name,

Diana Lesire Brandmeyer

Chapter 1 from a Time to Bake

Alison stepped out of the Sunshine Realty office, phone in hand. The sunlight bounced off the screen blinding her as she stepped into the street to cross to her car. The phone had dinged several times while she signed the contract on the small bakery she'd seen and had to have. It was exactly what she'd been dreaming about for years, and when two weeks ago she'd seen the For Sale sign. She knew in her soul this was the place she'd been dreaming about. Especially with rumors of more layoffs coming. Besides, there wasn't any reason to stay in St. Louis—

A horn blared.

Tires squealed.

Her breath caught as her feet cemented into the pavement. Then she was airborne. Time slowed. Everything around her went silent. Shouldn't she feel pain?

No, someone, a man had swept her up and now cradled her with strong arms under her legs. Her arms were wrapped around his neck. When had she done that? She looked up to thank him.

His eyes were the color of her favorite dark chocolate expresso icing, and his dark eyelashes framed them so well. Longings she'd buried for years surfaced. Her breath caught.

"What's wrong with you? Don't you know it's dangerous to text and walk? Especially when you're crossing a street? You could have been run over."

Was he shaking or was it her?

A car door slammed. Feet pounded and stopped next to her. "Hey, is she okay? I didn't hit her, did I?"

"I'm fine. You can put me down." At last, she found her voice. "Thank you for saving me. You're right. I shouldn't have been looking at my phone. My mind was on work and—" Her feet hit the ground. She swayed and caught hold of the man who'd scooped her from death.

"You're not fine." He steadied her, wrapping her in his arms.

The teenage boy rubbed his face with both hands. "My dad is going to kill me. I wasn't driving fast or checking my phone." His face pale against his dark hair.

"You didn't hit me. I'm unsteady because I suppose my brain is allowing me to realize how close I was to getting hurt, and now I realize how that would have affected you too. I'm so sorry. Will you be okay? Should I call someone for you?"

"No. I'm hoping no one witnessed this. Dad will take away my driving privileges just because. I think I'll take off if that's okay? I mean you are alright, and your boyfriend did save you."

"He's not my—just go." There was no need to explain to him that she had no idea who the man standing next to her was. The boy wasted no time and disappeared in a flash.

"Can I let go of you now?"

"Yes." He released his grip, leaving an ache at the broken connection. She took a step back surprised at the feeling of loss, then dismissed it as a reaction to the situation. "It was kind of you to risk your own life."

"He wasn't going that fast. But I don't want to do that again, so put that phone away when you're walking. It's dangerous, and there's nothing important enough that can't wait to be read, watched, or texted until you're not moving. Don't make others responsible for your poor choices."

"You sound like my dad."

"Then I guess you've heard it before."

Were his eyes even darker? And were those flecks of gold? Had they met? He looked like someone...maybe, but she'd met so many people because of her job. "I have. It's just that my mind is so busy, I have trouble keeping up with what's going on around me and at work. Which reminds me, I have messages that I have to reply to. Don't worry, I'll stay in one place until I'm finished." She pointed to her black Charger. "In there, motor on only for the air conditioning."

"Good, because one rescue a day is all I can handle. Stay safe." He nodded and walked away.

"Wait. I didn't catch your name. How can I thank you?"

"No need."

He said something else, but she didn't catch it. One thing for sure, once she moved here she would find out who he was and give him a box of her best cupcakes.

Chad drove down the street, passing the spot where he'd rescued the woman. When he saw her walking out in front of that car, his adrenalin—or was it Boy Scout training?—kicked in. He hadn't even considered he could have been hurt or worse. He hadn't even thought about his son and how Doug would have reacted if something happened. All common sense had fled Chad's body, and he'd rushed to get her out of danger.

She was light as a feather.

Something about the woman wouldn't leave him alone. Her lips had been close enough to kiss. For some reason, he'd wanted to. And she was a stranger. What kind of messed up was that? This had to be Deni's fault. She'd pushed at him long enough that's he'd weakened, and she'd got him to go on a date, a miserable one. And that must be the reason all the what ifs that women bring to a man's life had started to pop up in his brain. Like, the one he was thinking about now. What would her lips feel like? And did the sweet vanilla smell come from her hair or her lip gloss?

He hoped she was safe, paying more attention to her surroundings than her phone. Maybe he should have stuck around and made sure she returned her phone calls while she was parked.

Turning up the radio, he tried to drown out the thoughts about her and the soft skin of her arms around his neck.

Alison settled a cup filled with pens into the box on her office desk. It was taking her longer than she thought to clear out her personal belongings. At least, security team hadn't come and packed everything for her and brought the box to the entrance. It was awful to watch when the company laid off Cheryl. The woman was in tears as they escorted her downstairs and told her to wait for her things. Why the need to embarrass a former employee that had served the company well ate at her gut. If she ever had to let someone go from the bakery, she intended to let her employees leave with dignity attached.

"Does this have anything to do with that guy that saved you?" Shelly, her manager, leaned against the desk. "That would make more sense to me than you buying a bakery. I know you like to build your relationships with sugar and butter. It's what's got you the top seller award several times with this office. But open a bakery? With no experience? It has to be the guy."

"No. Nothing. I told you. I don't even know his name, and I'd already signed the contract before he scooped me out of danger." The pink pushpins were hers, but would she need them in her new office? Maybe, but if she needed new ones she'd get the cute ones she'd seen on Etsy that were made like cupcakes. She slid them back into the drawer.

"I think you should talk to someone. It was a near death experience." Shelly took the cup of pens out of the box and held them close to her chest. "You had 24 hours to cancel that contract and you might have, if you hadn't gazed into—what did you call them? Those after-dinner-chocolate eyes?"

Did Shelly think by holding her pens hostage she wouldn't leave? "You just don't get it. I've worked since my teens to make sure there will be enough money for any emergency—"

"But—"

"Exactly. What good did it do? My bank account is fine, but this week they laid off five more sales reps. Five. I don't want to be number six on

Monday." She sucked in a breath and let it out slow. She didn't need to react with anger. "I'm done working for someone else. Wondering if this is the last day of work. It happened to my dad, and I vowed never to let that happen to me." She reached for the cup and then relaxed her arm to her side. "You can keep those. I won't be needing them."

"The company is going to miss you, and so am I."

"They'll hire someone else who will with your training become a drug rep wonder. Besides, you kept me on the road so much I was seldom here."

She picked up the box. "One more thing left to do: stop in at human resources and turn in my ID card. And then I'm off to live out my dream." And if "after dinner eyes" asked her out someday, she planned on saying yes and seeing if the man that held her in her dreams the last two weeks was anything like the one in real life. But Shelly didn't need to know that.

Get a Time to Bake at Amazon

Other Books by Diana Lesire Brandmeyer

Contemporary

A Time to Love Series Silverton Lake Romances

All in Good Time

A Time to Dance
A Time to Bake
A Time to Heal

Mind of Her Own
Hearts on the Road

Historical
The Festive Bride
The Honey Bride
From a Distance
A Bride's Dilemma in Friendship, Tennessee
Matchmaker Brides Collection
Rails to Love Collection

About the Author

CBA and ESPA Best Selling, Christian author, Diana Lesire Brandmeyer, writes historical and contemporary romances about women choosing to challenge their fears to become the strong woman God intends. *Author of Mind of Her Own, A Bride's Dilemma in Friendship, Tennessee, We're Not Blended-We're Pureed, A Survivor's Guide to Blended Families.*

Sign up for her newsletter and get the story about Sandra Anderson free!

Website/blog: DianaBrandmeyer.com
Facebook: dianalesirebrandmeyer/author

Made in the USA
Monee, IL
30 August 2020